Bedroom Bully

Also Available by Trista Russell

Dead Broke

Chocolate Covered Forbidden Fruit

Fly on the Wall

Going Broke

Bedroom Bully

TRISTA RUSSELL

POCKET BOOKS

New York   London   Toronto   Sydney

Pocket Books
A Division of Simon & Schuster, Inc.
1230 Avenue of the Americas
New York, NY 10020

Designed by Renata Di Biase

Manufactured in the United States of America

ISBN-13: 978-1-61523-954-2

This is dedicated to the most beautiful brown face, cutest little smile, and brightest eyes I have ever known. You are as sweet as pink cotton candy and my heart flutters when you call me "Mommy." "Twinkle Twinkle Little Star" sounds like a hit on the Billboard charts from your mouth.

I love you, Braelyn!

Bedroom Bully

JOURNAL ENTRY:

Audra

All the local drunken regulars were at the local bar watching a search for a maniac when Kayla shouted out, "I don't think I could ever be raped. I enjoy dick entirely too much." She took everyone's attention away from the television.

"I think everyone heard you," Jackie, her seemingly shy friend said while nudging her.

"I don't care. None of these cheap bastards bought my drinks"—she got even louder—"and they never do, so I don't have to act like a lady for anyone in here."

"Yeah, but you never know who's listening," Jackie said, "and hearing you say something like that about sex could plant a bad seed in one of their sick minds."

"So what? I haven't had any in a while," Kayla said and pointed at a man across the bar. "If I planted a seed in your mind, let me know, 'cause you can have it, baby." Everyone around the bar laughed.

I don't know if it was what I was drinking or the fact that I too was longing for sex, but I found myself pondering her statement about rape. I secretly agreed with her. I couldn't see someone having to force me to have sex. I love it. Unless it was the neighborhood crackhead. What puzzles me is how she made the connection between the news story and sex. She was a bona fide freak. We were all gathered at the bar with our eyes glued to the forty-two-inch plasma television watching a tragic story unfold in our backyards—literally. Some new faces were at the bar because they couldn't get to their houses. The Miami-Dade police had all streets within a ten-mile radius of the crime shut down as they vigorously searched for the maniac who shot and killed two police officers at a routine traffic check. Florida's turnpike was shut down, and police were randomly searching cars entering or leaving the Cutler Bay area. It was a hot mess on a Friday night.

Regularly scheduled television programming had been preempted all day. People were told to stay indoors, and those who lived in the area where the crime occurred were told to stay with friends or family until the situation was completely under control. It was crazy. I left work at five, took the train and a bus to get to my car only to be stuck in traffic for two hours because of some asshole with a death wish. He had to be suicidal, because as soon as they showed his picture on the news, a black man, everybody knew that the police would make Swiss cheese out of him the first chance they got.

"I wonder if they would've done all of this if he shot just the average person," Kayla asked her friend. "Those bastards would be at Dunkin' Donuts." A few of us laughed at that thought. Her ranting was nothing new; she came in all the time. We *all* gathered at this local watering hole several times a week like Christians meeting for Bible study. She always drank screwdrivers and she was always at the bar on Fridays at six thirty-five. I know because I get there at six fifteen.

I don't know how Sammie's became the hot spot for drinkers. It could be that drinks were always two-for-one, and the characters who walked through the door couldn't be found anywhere else, not even on soap operas. Tonight, a dude we all call Dirty Harry, because he is a white guy who always wears a cowboy hat, was there. I can always count on Harry to be there. It's sad but refreshing to see a familiar face. I also like seeing Anthony, a good-looking brotha who is a manager at some local office. He was better looking before he started having sex with half the women who hung out at the bar. Now he got one of them pregnant. Crystal, the sloppy drunk, has given all the male bartenders head. She always made sure to do a good job, so she expected more than just the two-for-one deal, but she was always too drunk to notice that she was still paying full price.

As we all know, the spirit of alcohol temporarily delays good judgment, so people around the bar go home together all the time, and then, "lo and behold," things are never the same again. You'll see Jamal and Tamika chatting it up week after week, then all of a sudden she'd rather stand up if the only seat at the bar is next to him. That's the result of the two-for-one special and a lonely Friday night.

I have also gotten caught up. The men of Omega Psi Phi used to stop by after some of their frat meetings on the first Saturday of every month. At times, it would be only four or five of them and other times it would rain purple and gold everywhere. The eye candy was sweet, and they would behave like dawgs, barking and hopping.

However, there was one guy in particular who caught my eye. I had nicknamed him Mr. Suave. He was very charming and I would have to change my underwear every time I saw him walk through my door. It was orgasmic. His essence just reeked sex. His dark brown chocolate eyes would stare at me from across the bar and would tell me just what he wanted. I hoped to God that he knew he could have it.

One glorious night seven months ago, it all came to fruition when I left my cell phone on the bar and went to the restroom. I returned to my phone and noticed a text message: "What color panties are you wearing?" It was from a number I didn't recognize.

"You have the wrong person," I replied.

Another text came in: "I beg to differ, Ms. Low-Cut Pink Shirt."

I glanced around the restaurant and bar in search of someone who knew me. "Who is this?" I asked.

"Answer my question and I'll answer yours."

I already had four tequila sunrises and probably needed to take my butt home, but oh, no. I wrote back, "Black . . . lace . . . thong."

"You look delicious."

"LOL! C'mon, for real, who is this?" I asked playfully.

"One of the bartenders said that you call me Mr. Suave." Before I could pick my mouth up off the floor, another message came in: "Allow me to introduce myself. My name is Darryl."

I couldn't believe that we were talking . . . texting . . . or whatevering. "Hi, I'm Audra."

"Nice name, but I'd rather continue calling you what I've called you in my mind for weeks."

I couldn't even look up at him. I just stared at my phone. "What's that?" I typed.

"Sexy as hell," he wrote to me again. "May I call you that?"

"Sure." I blushed and finally glanced over at him. He was staring at me.

"May I join you?" he asked.

I could already feel my lower lips throbbing. "Yes, you may," I typed, fighting to be polite.

Darryl was six one or two, athletic build, dark chocolate, with striking and unique features and perfectly aligned pearly white teeth. He was handsome, smooth, and sexy. He was wearing khaki slacks, a beige shirt, and a speckled brown tie. I wondered how long I could wait before that tie was dangling in my face as he sweated on top of me.

He came over and sat next to me. We talked, and I blushed as the right corner of his upper lip curled when he smiled. I had a feeling we'd be lying naked somewhere together before midnight. Now, I don't make a habit of sleeping with strangers. But this guy had captivated my mind for weeks without ever speaking a single word to me, so I had to be honest with my body.

I didn't resist him that evening or any other evening since then. Darryl takes full control during sex. He doesn't "let" me do anything; he tells me what he wants me to do and I do it. I have these naughty fantasies of being forced, so he is perfect. He spanks me and likes me to call him Daddy. I love it! He roughs me up and puts it down hard-core like he is overdosing on Viagra pills.

Whenever we were done drinking, talking, and flirting, we were naked. As we spent time together outside of each other's bedrooms, he recognized a good woman in me. Darryl was 75 percent what I was looking for in a man. He was good-looking, independent, employed, and educated, and we were sexually compatible. Problem? That other 25 percent. He had a girlfriend, a fear of commitment, was as selfish as a three-year-old with no siblings, and could express his feelings only when he was drunk. We've been together seven months now, and for the last five months he's been making up excuses for why he can't leave his girlfriend yet encouraging me to hold on. "It'll be just me and you soon enough. I'm working on it. Just let me do what I have to do, but don't leave me," he kept saying. The minute I found myself believing him I knew that I was playing myself.

It was now after eleven and the bar was crowded. Everybody seemed to be there except Darryl, who had promised he'd meet me for drinks. It seemed the more often we saw each other in private, the less I saw him at Sammie's, which told me that he was probably "relating" with some other chick who is normally in there. I sent him several messages throughout the night asking him to come over, until he finally wrote back to say he wasn't on his way and didn't know what time he would be. I text-messaged him back, "Fuck you."

"Here you go, Henry." I handed over my bill and forty dollars. "Keep the change." I headed out the door. The night air was awesome, but that's every night in Florida. I was feeling all the drinks I had and desperately wanted to be cooped up under a man tonight—my man, or at least the one I was sharing. Damn, I was angry. My vibrator would hit the spot, but not like him.

I couldn't cry to my best friend, Casey. She'd say, "As I've said a million times, fuck Darryl. Call somebody else. I don't know why you waste your time with his ass anyway, he doesn't even like black women. He's not gonna leave that Spanish chick for you. Can't you see that?"

She's right, but I would never tell her that. I was faithful to Darryl because I hoped that someday he'd choose me. I ignored the fool he was making out of me every day. I went into our relationship knowing about his girlfriend. I thought I could handle it since our relationship was purely sexual. But now that I've turned the page and fallen for him, I get physically ill when I know that they're together. However, all it takes is for him to tell me he loves me. Then my heart is tranquilized and I'm willing to wait another day.

On my drive home, Casey called. "Wow, you answered! Let me guess, Darryl is nowhere to be found?"

Of course, I was upset but I tried to play it off. "I have better things to do."

"Like what, masturbate?" She laughed. "I don't know when you're going to find you a real man and drop Darryl's part-time ass."

"I've never had a problem *finding* a man," I informed her.

She teased, "Okay, then, find one tonight and let him blow that back out a lil' bit."

"Why?" I giggled. "I'm not about to catch crabs to prove anything to you."

"You need to prove some shit to yourself," she said.

"Whatever!" I shook my head.

Casey started talking and my mind zoned out. I've never in my life had a problem getting a man, even with these couple of extra pounds on me. I'm *still* pure fire. Dick was and will always be just a phone call, a text message, and or a knock on a door away, and much like Domino's Pizza it could be delivered to me in thirty minutes or less. However, I couldn't bring myself to have sex with anyone other than Darryl. To be honest, on nights like this, I have allowed a friendly young brotha to bless me with his tongue, but nothing more.

Casey was still talking about some sale at Macy's. "Hey, I have to go," I told her. "I'm pulling up to my place and have to take all of my work things in."

"All right, but be sure to lock up behind yourself. You know that psycho killer guy is still on the run."

"I can't believe a brotha done some crazy mess like that."

"He's kinda cute," Casey said. "You saw the pictures of him?"

"Hello! He's a murderer," I reminded her.

"They want his ass bad too; they got everything on lock trying to get his ass. He is as good as dead anyway. It's an eye for an eye; even if he surrenders they're going to kill him for killing those cops."

"Yep." I parked my car. "All right, girl, I'll call you tomorrow."

"Peace," she said. "Go get your double-A battery on."

"Shut up." I laughed.

I grabbed my purse, then popped the trunk and rounded the car to get all of the things I needed to do my work over the weekend. The last thing I took out was my rolling laptop carrying case. I started humming J. Holiday's "Bed." I loved that song, plus it was playing one of the last times Darryl and I were together, and that was exactly what he did: put me to bed. I hadn't seen him in a week, and I was missing him like a mother separated from her newborn baby. Though I had cursed at him via text message, I already knew that I would call him another three or four times before I went to sleep.

As I pushed my key into the lock, I felt a strong hand on my side. I automatically smiled. *My baby hadn't forgotten me.*

"Don't say a word, don't scream, and I won't hurt you." That voice didn't belong to Darryl.

I jumped. "What?"

"Don't talk. Just open the door," he instructed me.

"What do you want?" My hands dropped and the keys dangled in the doorknob. "Please don't do this to me."

"Just open the door, lady." He made his gun visible.

"Oh, my God." Tears came. "Please don't hurt me."

"Just open the fuckin' door," he said angrily.

As I turned the key, I remembered an episode of *Oprah* where the self-defense instructor harped on never allowing someone to take you to a second location. The second location is where you are raped and or killed. The second location is where your body will be found. I turned the knob pushed the door open quickly and twisted to run, only to double over and trip on my own damn laptop bag. "What the fuck are you doing?" He looked down at me. "Get up and get in there!" He pointed the gun at me.

I heard someone talking on a cell phone a few feet away around the corner. I needed to buy time so that she could see me, or him, or the gun. "Please, you can go inside and take whatever you want." I pretended to bargain. "I'll tell you exactly where my money is."

He was irritated. "Get in there." The gun made a clicking sound I had heard only on TV, and it always meant that the person it was aimed at needed to move his ass. So I did.

JOURNAL ENTRY:

Dean

I thought about tossing the gun, but it had gotten me this far. My heart was pounding, and my sweaty palms could hardly grasp the gun. I feared something would take over my mind and I might slip into psycho killer mode. That couldn't happen. I was still Dean Tyson, thirty-seven years old, educated, and a loving father. I was *still* me, but somehow I had fucked up. I would never have thought I was capable of shooting any one. Why did I do it today?

"Sit down," I told the woman, pointing to the sofa in her living room. "Is anyone else in here?"

"I live alone." She sat down with her hands held up like I was a bank robber. "You can have all of my jewelry and money," she begged. "I won't call the police if you take it and just leave."

"You can put your hands down," I said.

She lowered her hands but kept crying and running her mouth. "I'll even give you my ATM pin number, you can—"

"Shut up," I blurted out.

"You can withdraw everything."

"Shut the fuck up!" I shouted even louder. "I don't want your money, jewelry, or your ATM card," I said. "I just need to sit here in silence for a minute, until I figure out what to do next."

Finally, she was quiet. She said she lived alone but I made her walk me through the entire condo to be sure no one was in the house. The first bedroom was converted into an office. The walls were caramel brown and it was extremely organized. The second room was also neat and what I guess was the guest bedroom. The third room was her room. It wasn't as tidy as the rest of the house, but it was still nice.

"Sorry, I didn't make my bed this morning." She seemed a bit embarrassed even with these circumstances. "I was running late and just threw things around." She was crazy. Did she forget I had a gun?

"Get back to the sofa," I said.

"I mean, I could clean it up if you like."

"For what?" I asked. I wasn't going to leave her in there alone.

"To make things nicer here for you," she answered with a nervous smile. "Maybe it'll help to take you to a happier place and time."

I had to laugh. "I am not a nutcase."

"Maybe it'll help you think." She kept reaching. "You said you needed to think about something, right?"

"I'm sure you're an educated woman, but don't try that

psychology bullshit on me right now." I ushered her back to the living room. "I'm educated as well; I'm not some thug."

"Shit me." She got slick. "You're here to rob me. I can't tell."

"Number one, I'm not robbing you," I corrected her. "I don't need your shit and I've said that to you over and over again. I don't want your money. I just fucked up really bad today and need somewhere to be right now."

She sat silently across from me on the love seat. Finally I had a chance to think.

"You're that guy they're looking for, aren't you?" she said.

"What?"

"Are you Dean Tyson?"

"Oh, shit!" I fell back against the seat. "How do you know my name?"

"Well . . ." she hesitated. "It's been on the news all day."

"What are you talking about?" Was I hearing her right?

"Oh, my God." She looked increasingly frightened of me. "You killed those cops on the turnpike."

"I didn't *kill* anybody. I shot at them."

"Well, they're dead."

"C'mon." I laughed. "I think I might have gotten the first one in the leg and the other in the arm."

"They died," she announced.

"They're not dead." I didn't believe her. "I didn't kill anybody."

"Those men died." She pointed at the remote control on the table.

I turned to CNN, and, sure enough, even though it was close to midnight the reporter was working overtime. The headline read, "Manhunt, the Turnpike Cop Killer," right next to a picture of me. It was my MySpace profile picture.

The news reporter said the first cop was shot in the chest and died on the scene, and the second was hit in the upper thigh, near the femoral artery, and lost a massive amount of blood. He died on the helicopter that was airlifting him to the trauma center.

"What the fuck?" I said. The gun dropped into my lap. I had to hold my hands to my head because the room was spinning.

Suddenly I heard my neighbor Mrs. Lopez's voice on the television. "He is normally a very nice guy. He keeps to himself a lot." She paused. "He's been inside my house several times to fix things or help me with heavy objects." She started to cry. "Just thinking that my life was in danger all that time is scary."

"Are you fuckin' serious, Ms. Lopez?" I was pissed.

She went on with the interview. "When I saw him this morning there was something in his eyes that said hate, ya know? It was like he wanted to hurt someone."

Yeah, but there was nothing hateful in my eyes two months ago when she grabbed my dick through my sweatpants and wanted me to put a "hurtin'" on her fifty-year-old pussy. Nothing was hurt besides her feelings when I turned her down. Now look at her.

Next up there was street newspaper vendor Hal. "Yeah, ah,

Dean is a good dude." He spoke with his regular Boston accent. "I see him most every mornin', right here on this corna. Taday was no different, he said good mornin' and bought a pappa." I hadn't bought a paper that morning. I guess he lied to paint a better picture of me. "He musta jus' snapped, ya know?"

I think my mind went black for several minutes. My friends and family were all probably going insane about this, but what was my baby girl thinking? Did Destiny think her father was crazy? What would happen to her now? Would I ever see her again? My profound thoughts were interrupted by Alicia Keys's "No One" blaring from the woman's cell phone.

JOURNAL ENTRY:

Audra

Alicia belted "No one, no one, no one" from inside my purse. My heart skipped a couple of beats because it was my ring tone for Darryl. I had an idea. "Do you want me to turn it off?" I asked Dean.

"Yeah," he said, then quickly changed his mind. "Naw. Actually, hand me the bag, I'll turn it off."

Well, there went my chance to dial 911. I handed the purse to him, and the phone started ringing again. "No one, no one, no one . . ."

He ransacked my bag and somehow Darryl was on speakerphone. "Baby?" he said. "You there?"

Dean eagerly motioned for me to respond. "Hey!" I said.

"So what's the problem tonight?" He was ready to argue.

"You know that we were supposed to meet at Sammie's. Where are you?" I asked. I always asked this but never knew what was a true or false answer from him. He'd be in Chicago and tell me he was in Tallahassee. He'd say he was in Orlando when he was really in Key West or right down the damn street. He never allowed one person to know too much about him at all. Not only did he loathe being vulnerable, but that would trigger his commitment phobia. What a keeper I had!

"I'm on my way to your place," he said. "I miss you, baby."

Even in the midst of being a hostage I was still falling for Darryl's shit. "Really?" I blushed.

"Yes, baby, I love you." I could tell he had been drinking. "You know that?"

"I love you too." I was still cheesing.

"Even though you like starting drama all the damn time." He laughed. "What was that 'fuck you' text message all about?"

"You know what it was all about!" I said sternly.

"Enlighten me." He chuckled.

I tried to prolong the conversation, expecting Dean to disconnect at any second. "I thought I was going to see you earlier tonight."

"With 'thought' being the operative word. You *thought* wrong. I had already told you that that wasn't likely, Audra." He was a real jerk sometimes.

I was embarrassed that someone else was hearing the way I allowed him to talk to me. "You can be such an ass, Darryl."

"Dammit, baby, don't start that shit tonight. You know that I have to put in my time with her on Friday nights so that my weekends are free," he said.

"You must've put in your time with her every night. I

haven't seen you and hardly heard from you this whole week." I really didn't intend to say all of that in front of a stranger, but when a woman's fed up . . .

"We'll talk when I get there. I'm on my way." Talk? Yeah, right. He knew that nine times out of ten his dick could and would rectify any situation. "I can't stay long, because I have to go see her and spend the night at her place. She's mad about some bullshit."

"Excuse me? Didn't you *just* say that you were with her already tonight?" I asked. "You are such a liar, Darryl." I wanted to burst out in tears. "Don't bring your ass over here. I have company."

"Company?" He was shocked. "Company? Who?"

"Does it matter?" I asked. "I should've started having company a long time ago. I take a backseat to Jasmine every fuckin' day and I'm sick of it."

"Baby, I put you first whenever I can." His drunken voice slurred. "Let's talk about this when I get there. My battery's dying." He always had an excuse to end a phone call whenever I wasn't saying things to glorify him. "I'll be there soon."

Dean was shaking his head. "You can't come here, Darryl," I repeated.

"Why the hell not?" he shouted.

"I told you—I have company. Not tonight."

He went quiet for a few seconds. "Are you serious?"

"Yes. I have someone over and I'm not opening my door for you." It felt good to say that to him. "Darryl, I can't keep waiting on you to choose me, so I made a choice for myself, and he's here." With that said, Dean ended the call and I turned off my phone. I pouted for the next five minutes and Dean sat staring in my direction. I'm sure he didn't give a damn about me and my "man" problem. He was in much deeper doo-doo. A couple of tears leaked out of my eyes. "May I go get some Kleenex?" I asked.

"No," he answered, but it appeared as though he didn't really hear me.

"Can you get it for me, then?" I had tears, eyeliner, mascara, and snot hardening on my face.

"No," he replied.

To hell with that! I was fed up with all men now. I stood and sauntered my ass right past him and down the hall to my room. When my fingers touched the doorknob, his hand was around my neck pulling me back toward the living room. "Didn't I say no?" He pushed me over to the sofa. "This is no time to be bold, woman."

"I need to clean my face." Suddenly something came out of my mouth that shouldn't have. "I'm not afraid of you. Just like you didn't mean to kill those cops, I know you're not going do anything to me, so whatever!"

Dean gave me a look so evil that the devil would tremble. "Because those cops are dead I can do whatever the fuck I please. A life sentence is a life sentence. If they give me ten I can still only serve one. So don't take this shit lightly."

I was now lying on the sofa staring at the ceiling, wishing and hoping that Darryl heard something in my voice that triggered concern, knowing that a killer was on the loose, and he had called the police. However, after thirty minutes passed, I realized that he was probably glad to be rid of me. Jasmine was probably scratching his back up and screaming, "Fuck me, Papi!" somewhere fifteen miles away. The thought made my stomach lining rush up toward my mouth, as it did every time I knew he was making love to her.

Bam! Bam! Bam! Knuckles were beating on my front door. Dean and I looked at each other. He pointed the gun at me and motioned for me to stand up. I seriously didn't know who could be at my door at this hour of the night if it wasn't Darryl, but Darryl was too proud to be told not to come over and do it anyway. You couldn't tell him anything you truly didn't mean. Dean walked with me to the door, and I looked through the peephole. It *was* Darryl.

"It's him," I whispered.

"Audra, open the door," Darryl said. "I know you're up; I see the light."

"What do you want me to do?" I asked.

"Will he go away if you don't answer?" Dean looked confused.

"He might, but you turned my phone off. He's probably been trying to call me." I wanted him to let me open the door. "Maybe if I just go out and talk to him he'll leave."

"Do you think I'm stupid?" he asked.

"Well, what do you want me to do?"

"Audra!" Darryl got louder and louder. "Open the door."

I had never heard him so eager for my attention. "He's going to wake up the neighbors," I lied. The people next door had moved out the week before.

"Open it," Dean instructed, "but talk to him with the chain on. If you give him any signal or signs I'll"—he paused and looked me dead in the eyes—"I'll hurt you."

"Okay." I was scared. "What do you want me to say?"

"Just get rid of him," he said. "Tell him that you have company, just as you did over the phone."

"Okay." Before I unlocked the door I unbuttoned my shirt. Dean looked perplexed. "What are you doing?"

"I'm supposed to have company, right?" I smiled.

It was another lie. I really wanted my shirt open so that I could signal to Darryl with my left hand. Dean was standing on my right behind the door.

"Audra." Darryl knocked again.

I opened the door. "What are you doing here?"

"I told you I was coming," he said with a smile as he noticed my opened blouse. "Damn, I love your tits, baby. I'm glad you ready, 'cause I'm dying to suck on them nipples."

"Sorry, but I have company, Darryl, as I told you." I widened my eyes to signal something was wrong, but he wouldn't look away from my breasts.

"Stop playing the drama queen role with this 'company' bullshit." He pushed the door to get in and was stopped by the chain. "What are you doing? Open the door."

"Darryl." I shaped my fingers to look like a gun and held it up so Dean couldn't see. "I have company."

"You won't have anybody up in there with you." Darryl, for the first time ever, seemed jealous. "You won't do me like that, Audra."

"I'm tired of being lonely. You've been promising to break up with Jasmine now for months." I kept trying to make him look at my fingers, but he wouldn't. "I can't take that anymore."

He pushed the door again, and this time Dean got annoyed. He pulled off his shirt and stepped to the other side of me, gently pushing me aside, and removed the chain from the door. He kept the gun hidden behind the door as he confronted Darryl. "Look, bro, she asked you not to come over in the first place, right? So what's the problem?"

"Who the fuck are you?" Darryl asked.

"That's not important." Dean was maneuvering his face away from the light sneaking in through the doorway. "What is important is that you get home safely, 'cause it sounds like you've had one too many drinks."

"Don't tell me what the fuck I've had." Darryl looked over at me. "Who in the hell is this guy?"

"Let's talk when you've sobered up some, Darryl," I said, trying to keep him calm. "I'll call you tomorrow."

"Naw." He shook his head. "Don't call me tomorrow, don't call me Sunday or any other goddamn day. I'm not *on call*."

All the months I wasted being runner-up flashed before my eyes. My rage vomited through my mouth. "You're not *on call*? That's funny because that's all I ever was for you—on call, like a damn emergency room nurse. The only time you call me is when no one else shows up. So fuck you!" Dean didn't have to close the door; I slammed it.

I felt like a cancerous growth had just been removed from my body. I was through with Darryl's heartless, selfish, inconsiderate ass.

I marched off to my room. "Dean, just shoot me." I needed a moment and I was taking it. I pounced onto the bed and buried my head in my pillow. Though I couldn't find it in me to cry another tear for Darryl, my heart felt like I was weeping heavily. In deepest of thought I removed all the layers that made up Darryl and revealed that he was just a good fuck. There was no substance to him, no conversation, nothing to respect, no future, no joy, no commitment, no financial stability, no security, nothing. There was nothing to him, but I had mistakenly allowed him to grow on me.

"Hey!" I had heard Dean enter into the room minutes before he said anything. "I know that you're a little sensitive right now, but because of *my* situation I can't let you be back here by yourself." I didn't care if he saw my weakness; I wasn't about to pretend to be strong. Plus, he was the one with the gun. He knew I was powerless. "Are you okay?" he asked.

I hesitated. "Yeah, I'll be fine."

"Okay." He wasn't leaving the room. "I'll chill over here on this La-Z-Boy, and you can stay in the bed and get some rest, or sleep if you want."

"Thanks." Did he think I did time in a penitentiary or something? I couldn't sleep with guns and shit nearby. Sleep?

There was no way I was going to be able to sleep in the same room with a man wanted for murder and holding the murder weapon in his hand just a few feet away from me. "What about you?" I asked. "Are you going to sleep?"

"Naw, too much on my mind." He chuckled, "I guess I'll sleep when I'm in prison." He paused. "Or dead."

We were both quiet for a while. I looked at the clock and it was after two in the morning. I broke the silence. "So . . . why did you do it?"

"Do what?" Dean asked back.

"Kill those officers." I was straight up.

"I told you, I didn't kill them." He shook his head. "I shot them."

"Why did you shoot them?" I didn't want to anger him, but I had to know.

"I had somewhere I needed to be." He said it as though it was all so simple.

"Was it worth it?"

He shrugged. "I still haven't made it to where I was going."

"Still wanna go?" I asked.

"Yeah," he answered. "More than ever now."

I tried getting personal with him. "And where exactly is that?"

"What's your name?" he asked, changing the subject.

"Audra. Audra Chandler."

"Audra, no more questions," he said adamantly. "Get your rest."

"I will, but I do have a rather serious question to ask before

I can get comfortable enough to close my eyes with you in this room."

"Go ahead." He was losing patience.

"I have done everything that you've asked me to do," I stated. "If I continue to follow whatever you say, are you going to hurt or kill me regardless?"

"No." He took a deep breath. "My intention was never to kill those men. I am not a murderer or some out-of-control crazy maniac." He hung his head. "The man they are searching for isn't Dean Tyson, and I know that because I am Dean Tyson." He looked over at me with what looked like tears frozen on the windowpanes of his eyes. "As long as you do exactly what I tell you to do, everything should be okay."

"All right." I sighed. "Well, I won't lie. I still don't think that I can sleep with a gun in such close proximity."

"Try!" he said dryly. "Because it's not going anywhere."

JOURNAL ENTRY:

She read, or at least stared at, the pages of a book most of the night and looked at me out of the corner of her eyes the rest of the time. I'm sure that she was sleepy because there were several times I nearly gave in to the bricks on my eyelids. I needed at least an hour of sleep to be functional the next day, but I couldn't close my eyes for longer than a blink in her presence. I knew she would pull a Carl Lewis as soon as I gave her a chance.

I was exhausted, and when the clock read seven I gave up. "Hey," I said to her, "I need you to get up."

"Why?" She closed her book. "Is something wrong?"

"Do you have mittens?"

"We live in Miami."

"You're a woman. Women always buy shit they don't need." She probably had a scarf and earmuffs too.

"Maybe. Why?"

"I also need a couple pairs of panty hose."

"Why?"

"Just get them." She pulled out the items from her closet.

I told her to put on the mittens and go into the bathtub.

I grabbed the panty hose and used them to tie up her hands and legs.

"What the hell?" She began to panic. "You said you wouldn't hurt me." She was about to cry.

"I'm putting you in here because there is something I have to do." I put several folded towels on the bottom of the tub so she would be comfortable and sat her down.

"How long are you leaving me in here?"

"Not long, don't worry." I lied. "Since these are nylons, the more you wiggle the tighter they'll get, so just sit tight."

"What are you going to do?"

Her dark brown puppy dog eyes glared up at me. "I don't understand why I'm being tied up like, like . . . like a fuckin' animal and you're telling me not to worry about it."

I decided to sleep sitting up against the door. Well, at least that's how I started out. When I woke up, I was laid out on the carpet. The clock on her nightstand showed it was after ten. I panicked. I had been asleep for nearly three hours.

I slowly opened the door to the bathroom. She was still sitting just as I had positioned her. "Are you okay?" I asked.

"Yeah, I'm wonderful," Audra said sarcastically.

I was starving. "What do you have here to eat?" I inquired.

"Not much," she said.

"Damn." I was hungry.

"I mean I have food, but nothing that you can consider a five-course meal." She thought more. "I think there is a frozen pizza in there too."

Desperate times called for desperate food. "That'll work," I said.

"Well, I'm hungry too but not for a frozen pizza," Miss Prissy informed me. "I can cook breakfast if you like."

"Are you any good?" I asked.

"I've never had a complaint," she said. "I'm pretty good, but one thing I am not good at is contortionism." She glared down at herself.

"Sorry." I couldn't imagine how uncomfortable she was. "I heard you trying to get out of here," I lied.

"I doubt you could hear anything over your snoring." She chuckled.

"Snoring?" I tried to play it off. "What snoring?"

"It was pretty obvious that you were asleep. I was screaming for you every five minutes because I needed to use the toilet." She looked down at her lap. "Now I need to take a shower. I couldn't hold it."

I took that to mean that she had peed on herself. At least I hope that was all she had done. "I'm sorry about that. I'll get these things off of you." I moved toward her and started to I untie the panty hose from her ankles and the faucet.

"May I take a shower?" she asked.

Sure. I grimaced as I smelled her. She seemed embarrassed. "I'm sorry about not hearing you."

"Not a problem, as long as I can wash up." I untied her and she started stretching.

"Are you going to continue running or turn yourself in and tell them that you didn't mean to do it?"

"Do you know how many people are in jail for doing something they didn't *mean* to do?" I said. "Nobody *means* to do anything bad, but the law remains the same."

"Yeah, but maybe when they hear your story—"

I interrupted her. "You don't even know what my story is. Let me worry about all that. Take your shower and hurry up."

"Sure," she snapped, "as soon as I have some privacy."

"This is as private as it gets." I leaned up against the vanity.

"Excuse me?" She gave me attitude. "You're not leaving?"

"You can close the curtain, but I have to stay," I said. "I can't take any chances."

"You left me in here before!"

"You were tied up."

"There isn't even a window in here, you know."

I was aware of that, but I was even more aware of the fact that there were things in the bathroom she could use to try and hurt me, like bleach, razors, sharp tweezers, etc. She couldn't be left alone. "This is not about seeing you naked, been there and done that—plenty," I said. "I'm not leaving you in here alone."

She angrily pulled the shower curtain closed. A few seconds later her clothes went flying everywhere, except her bra and panties.

The bathroom became a sauna. The fruity smell of her shower gel become intoxicating. Suddenly all I could think about was her sliding slippery slices of mango all over her wet body, which I wanted to see. I quickly opened the bathroom door to let out some of the steam, smell, and lustful thoughts.

"Would you like me to leave the water on for you?" she asked innocently.

"Umm." I thought about it. I desperately needed a shower; I should've taken one the day before. "Yeah, sure, leave it on."

She poked her hand out and pointed behind me. "Pass me a towel, please." I handed her one from the neatly folded stack.

I took off my shirt, shoes, and then my pants, and was standing there in just my briefs when she pulled back the curtain wearing the towel. It was an Uncle Jesse "Have mercy" moment. The towel didn't cover anything. I could see creamy milk chocolate breasts protruding from the sides of her towel, and her legs were as smooth as silk.

This wasn't the time or place for me to be thinking about sex, but I was a man before I was anything else. I'm also a man who had sex with a skinny woman once and vowed never to stick my dick into another cadaver again for as long as I live. I like something to hold on to. Since then I've dated only women with meat on them—not less than 160 pounds. Audra was about five seven and hovering close to 180 pounds. She was well proportioned, with a beautiful face like Toccara from *America's Next Top Model*. Her plush velvety brown skin peeked at me and seemed to have my name written all over it. I was willing to bet money that the nipples on her 38 or 40 DDs were large, and suddenly I wondered what they would feel like expanding in my mouth.

She tried nonchalantly to glance at my chest and my thighs, but when her eyes rounded my somewhat swollen dick she broke the awkward silence. "So what do you want me to do?"

In my mind I answered, *I want you to let that towel drop so I can see those tig ole bitties, baby.* I was truly in awe. I hadn't looked at her as a woman until right then. My adrenaline had truly played a trick on me the day before. It's amazing what a little sleep could do. I couldn't stop staring at her face. She was drop-dead gorgeous, even without makeup and designer clothing.

"What do you want me to do," she asked again, "while you're in the shower?"

"Oh!" I uttered as my spaceship landed back on Earth. However, my brain was still on planet Stickmydickbetween-yourtits. "You'll try to run, won't you?"

"No, I promise I won't run." She tried to sound convincing, but her wide-eyed look said that she'd be screaming in the street in that pale pink towel. I couldn't help chuckling at her Academy Award–winning act.

"You can sit right there on the toilet while I take my shower." I smiled and closed the bathroom door.

"What makes you so sure that I won't run as soon as you pull the curtain?" she asked as she took her assigned seat.

"Because I'm not pulling the curtain." I removed my briefs. Now, because there was no history or chemistry between us, I was a tad self-conscious about my penis. There was no reason for her to look at what I had and say, "Damn, sign me up!" My shit didn't hang down to my knees like those on the brothas in most of those romance novels in her room probably did. I had a solid and reasonably thick seven-incher that had made women squirt, scream, and squeal. However, more often than not they doubted that I would lay them out because of the 12-inch dick they read about in their books. I'm representin' for the average brothas. We can lay the wood, *baby*.

I grabbed a washcloth from the rack and almost rubbed up against her to get into the shower. She had her hand over her eyes so as to not invade my privacy. I rested the gun on a towel on the rack behind me and turned toward the shower-head. As the hot water slapped my chest I hurriedly glanced down to see how much of my skin was now missing. "Shit." I jumped out of the way of the stream.

"This shit is fire engine hot," I yelled.

"That's the way I like it." She smiled. As she leaned over to adjust the water temperature, her towel nearly slipped.

She was still trying to be a good girl by shielding her eyes, but I know I saw her take a peek at my goods.

"Is this fruity-smelling soap the only kind you have?" I didn't want to smell like a girl if I was going to prison.

"Yep," she said with a half smile. "Beggars can't be choosers."

"I'm not begging."

"That's probably true, since you *are* the one with the gun," she said sarcastically.

"I just don't beg." I grabbed the soap and rubbed it on the wet washcloth, then moved it over my body. "You shouldn't have to beg for anything either, including your man's attention." Ms. Big Mouth didn't say a word in response.

I began lathering my face. When I opened my eyes all I saw was the pink towel disappear around the corner. I sprinted from the tub, wiping my face with my hand, and saw the towel on the floor and her naked body running down the hall toward the door. I caught up to her and snatched her hand away from the doorknob. She fell to the carpet, and I went down on top of her.

"Help! Help me, somebody," she screamed.

I put my hands over her mouth. "Don't do that," I said nervously. "Don't make me hurt you." In an instant I saw myself as a shackled inmate; there was no way I could have that type of future. I tightened my grip on her mouth.

She kept trying to scream, and then she bit the living shit out of my fingers.

"Dammit." I almost slapped her. I had never hit a woman, but I wanted to kill her.

"*Help me!*" she yelled again.

"Shut the fuck up or I will hurt you." I grabbed her by the neck. "I swear, don't fuckin' play with me." My freedom depended on her mouth. My heart raced and sweat beads pushed through my temple. I looked around the room for something to put in her mouth. I held her down with my weight and stuffed a balled shirt into her mouth. Tears slid down her face as she tried to push me off her. She bucked and pranced, but she wasn't going anywhere.

After a few long minutes she stopped, and I rested my knees on the carpet. I relaxed, and just as I remembered that we were both naked, she began to squirm beneath me again.

Her hardened nipples raked back and forth on my bare chest.

"Look, if you stop I'll let you up to get dressed," I promised her. I needed her to stop moving the way she was because it was affecting me in ways I could not afford to concentrate on at the moment. She thrashed her body about even more. Soon I had to use my thigh to open her legs so I could lie between them to hold her down. She wrapped her legs around mine and struggled with me, but she was stuck. The only thing that ended up happening was that my dick slapped into her pussy lips once or twice in the fight she was pursuing.

"You promised me you wouldn't run." I looked down at her. "Why would you do that? You knew I was gonna catch you."

"Ugggh," she groaned. "Mmmmmmm." Her words were muffled because of the shirt in her mouth.

"Just relax. I can outlast you, so save your strength."

She growled and shot me a dirty look.

She continued to try and push me off her by thrusting up her body weight. My dick was constantly rubbing her and I was losing the power struggle. I could tell that her pussy was shaved, and that was a major weakness for me. "Oh, God!" I whispered. It was my secret little prayer asking the Lord to stop the erection I felt coming on. "Please stop that," I begged her. "You're only going to make things hard." No pun intended.

She didn't and wouldn't stop. Her large breasts, chunky bald pussy, and solid ass continued to tantalize me. "Fuck!" I whimpered as my fully sharpened pencil was eager. "Damn."

I tried to show self-control but couldn't. I now had both of her hands held tightly with one hand. My other hand was on a slow trek down to one of her breasts, and against my better judgment I slid the backs of my fingers over her firm nipple. I played with it awhile before I palmed and squeezed her breast like a melon. "Look at what you're making me do," I said to her.

She mumbled something back and shook her head from side to side. She stared up at me in fear, and I'm sure she felt my rock-solid dick head resting on her pussy like a boulder up against the entrance of a cave. And boy was I Captain Caveman! I tried to keep my body still, but little Miss Wiggle Worm started up again, and the tip of my throbbing dick polished her clit and a grunt of enjoyment escaped me. Soon I found my lips on her neck and my fingers massaging her supple breast again. She squirmed beneath me more, causing her pussy to slide up and down the side of my chocolate stick.

"Audra." I remembered her name and used it to try to stop myself from nibbling on her neck but couldn't. "Please stop moving. My dick can only take so much. It's like you're grinding on me, I mean I know that you're not, but my dick can't tell the difference." I got my wits about me enough to look into her face and say, "Just stop moving like that and give me a minute to gather myself. It'll go down," I promised her, "and then I'll let you up."

Every man has a breaking point, and mine came just three seconds after I spoke to her. She started working that pussy like she wanted me to have it, so I let my fingers walk down between her thighs and placed her clit between my index and middle fingers and slowly grinded in small circles. She moved her body like she was still fighting me, which accidentally caused my middle finger to slip into her. "Oooooh shit," I exclaimed as her warm and wet walls enveloped my finger. "Fuck. You feel so damn good." I looked into her eyes and truly couldn't decipher her emotions.

I was now fingering her, rubbing her clit, and taking turns sucking on both her breasts. She was still going through the motions of growling and slowly bucking her body, but I was too busy enjoying her and oblivious to the fact that what I was doing could be against the law. Of course I could take the shirt out of her mouth and find out if I had her permission, but somehow it was a big turn-on not to know. I was in a sensual fog for a few minutes, and when it cleared I was fingering her so fast that her tight pussy had my whole hand wet.

I then allowed my dick head to bump up against her wet lips, but this time it was a whole new animal. I looked down into her face for a sign that begged me to stop and I saw none. I teased her entranceway. I wanted to give it to her. Who would stop me? She wasn't fighting as hard anymore, so she either wanted it or was tired. I pushed past her pussy's velvet rope and landed in the VIP section. I entered her. "Damn." I said it because of both the intense pleasurable feeling I was experiencing and what I had possibly done—committed yet another crime.

"Oh, shit. I'm sorry," I said. Was I raping her? I was disgusted with myself, the animal I had become and the good man I had stopped being. I pulled my dick out, released her hands, and took the shirt out of her mouth. I was ready for her to run and call the cops on me, or for her to start punching and screaming but instead she whimpered, "Don't stop." She reached beneath me and guided my dick back to her.

"Huh?" I was confused.

"Put it back in," she said.

"Are you sure?" I had to be certain.

"Yes." She moaned, and as quickly as she answered I plunged back in.

"I thought I was . . ." I didn't want to use the word "rape." "Umm, thought maybe I was violating you," I said.

"Maybe you were, maybe you weren't." She groaned. "But you feel so good . . . take this pussy." She put her hands back up over her head and said, "Hold me down and rough me up again."

My dick was even harder now. "You really want me to take it, huh?"

"No!" she said, playing through her clenched teeth, but she was soon moaning loudly as I began giving her that aggressive dick she begged for. For about ten minutes or so she pretended to fight me, push me off, and was even still saying no and begging me to stop.

"No." I thrust deeper and deeper. "Fuck me back."

"You said you wouldn't hurt me," she cried.

"I'm not hurting you." I bent one of her legs upward so I could get in all the way. "You wanted me to take it, so I'm taking it."

"Oh, yes, take it, Dean." She couldn't pretend anymore.

"You like that?"

"Yes!"

"So fuck me and stop playing this game," I said as I flipped her onto her stomach to hit that sweet pussy from behind. "Fuck me, Audra." I slid my dick back into her sweetness, and she truly could no longer act as if she wasn't enjoying it. She went from zero to sixty in one second, backing that juicy, plump, warm hole up on me like she had something to prove. "That's good shit, baby." She felt so good, and I couldn't believe that I was inside of her, a stranger. "Damn, girl, yeah." I felt my load coming. I wanted to hold it off, but it had been awhile and this was too good. "I'm about to bust . . ."

"Wait, wait, not yet . . . hold on!" she said.

"Ooooh, shit. I'm coming." I pulled out of her and my cannon shot its load straight out onto the sofa. "Damn."

JOURNAL ENTRY:

Audra

You know that does-anyone-one-else-do-this? guilty feeling you get after you masturbate while watching some bizarre porn you stumbled upon on the Internet? Well, multiply that by ten, add one hundred, and carry the two, and that should pretty much sum up what I'm feeling. Why? I just stopped a murderer from adding rape to his rap sheet by willingly giving my goods to him. All because he's handsome and has a slamming body and a well-defined dick head that made my pussy water. I just had sex with a murderer and I loved it. Now here I am, facedown on the carpet, panting and ashamed.

"Here you go." I felt something warm touch my back. I looked over and he was handing me a washcloth.

"Thanks," I said as I took it.

"I thought you might want this too." He held open the pink towel I had been wearing earlier.

I didn't know what to think or feel about him. "I need to use the bathroom."

"Go ahead." With a towel around his waist he lay down on my sofa.

I closed the bathroom door and, to keep my sanity, blamed my state of mind on the things that Darryl had put me through. Like how he knew how to make me keep holding on. He'd talk about every argument with Jasmine to give me hope, and two seconds later he'd start telling me about how in love he was. What about me? Darryl had absolutely nothing to do with what went down in my living room, but it made me feel better to have an excuse.

I took another shower and was surprised Dean didn't come in to monitor me. But why would he? He's already seen and felt everything I was supposed to be hiding. I left the shower running and quietly opened the door to the cabinet under the sink. I was in search of a steak knife I had placed in there for some crazy reason. "Yes!" I whispered as I found it behind my disorganized clutter of cleaning products.

I placed the knife in my dirty clothes, turned off the shower, dried myself, and was stunned to see Dean with the gun pointed at me outside of the bathroom door when I opened it. "Put your clothes on the floor," he demanded.

"I was about to put them in the laundry basket in my room," I told him.

"Okay. Just let me take a look at them first."

Dammit, I was caught! I could pull it out and go after him, just show him, or put it down and let him discover it on his own. "Fine." I dropped the bundle and watched the knife expose itself, then walked into my room like his gun didn't make a difference.

"Damn." He followed me into the room. "I thought that I had just made a friend," he said.

"And what would make you think that?" I turned and asked.

"Nothing." He smirked. "Nothing at all."

Still covered by my towel, I put on my panties and shuffled to get into my bra. I lowered a sundress over my head, pulled the towel down, and asked, "Do you still want breakfast?"

"Sure, minus the poison, crushed glass, and microscopic metal pieces." He shook his head. "No, thank you. I think I'll pass."

"Fine," I said. "Do you mind if I make something for myself?"

"No." He paused. "But I *do* mind you being around all of those knives."

"I wasn't going to do anything with the knife."

"So why did you have it so conveniently folded up in your shirt?"

"Maybe because you're walking around with a damn gun." I looked up at his terribly handsome face and thought of the way he had just handled my body. "I'm not going to run."

"I've heard that before," he scoffed. "I can't take that chance."

"Look, I don't condone what you've done. I don't know why you did it, but I do think that if you were going to hurt me you would've already." I continued, "Do I want you in my house? No I don't, and especially not with a gun. So let's make a deal."

"What?" he asked.

"If you put the gun away I'll promise not to run or do anything stupid, and you can stay here and continue to sort things out until tomorrow morning. Okay?"

He thought it over for a couple seconds, "Where would I put it?"

"I bought a fireproof lockbox a few weeks ago. I've never set a combination on it, so you can put it in there and make your own combination. Then only you will have access to it."

"And you will let me stay until tomorrow morning." He wanted to be clear. "And you give me your word not to run?"

"I've given you a whole lot more than just my word, Mr. Tyson," I said. "But yes, I give you my word."

He took a deep breath. "Where's the security box?"

I sighed as I walked to the closet to get the box. I couldn't believe that I had talked him into it, but more than anything I couldn't believe that I was truly going to keep my word.

He grabbed the box, read the instructions on the top, and then placed the gun, my cell phone, and the steak knife inside. "You wanna go get the others?" he joked.

"I gave you my word," I said.

He spun the numbers around, pressed the button on the side, spun them again, and closed the box. He checked the handle and it was locked. "Does your man have any clothes here?" he said, looking down at the towel.

I went to the drawer where I kept Darryl's left-behind be-longings. "Try these." I threw a pair of shorts and a T-shirt his way.

He put them on and looked better than Darryl even did in them. "Thanks."

"No problem," I said. "So may I cook now?"

"Naw," he replied. "I think I'll do the cooking."

"Are *you* any good?" I mocked him as I followed him into the kitchen.

"Didn't the reporters mention that I am the executive chef at a restaurant in the Gables?" He looked back at me and winked. "So I am very good."

"I'll be the judge of that."

I showed him where everything was and watched him work. He wasn't a chef who needed special cutlery or pans. His cooking looked rather simple, but my house had never smelled so delicious. I almost wanted to lick the walls. "Do you have orange juice?" he asked.

"Yes."

"Since you can't cook, you can pour two glasses." He laughed. "Please."

"I *can* cook," I said as I filled the glasses. "Someone else just wanted to show off."

"How about toast, can you manage that?"

"I can make a mean toast," I joked.

"Hook it up, then."

In about ten minutes he set a plate in front of me with the fluffiest omelet I had ever seen, along with my toast, and slices of strawberries. No omelet that had ever graced my stove looked so good. It had bacon, bell peppers, tomatoes, and cheese.

Surprisingly, while we were eating neither of us said a word. I was in deep thought about what had happened earlier. I kept telling myself that *cannot* happen again.

When I was done eating, I watched the television to avoid in his eyes. It took awhile for me to realize that it wasn't on. When I turned toward him, I caught him staring, but he quickily dropped his eyes and reached for my plate. "You all done?"

"Yes, thanks. It was scrumptious."

As Dean began to wash the dishes, I said, "It's Saturday and I'm sure my mother has tried to call me. If I don't call her soon, she will knock down that door." And that was the truth.

"Maybe later. But it'll have to be on speakerphone."

"No problem." I clicked on the television. The news was still talking about him. I quickly changed the channel.

"Put it back," he said.

It was noon, so golf or something should've been on, but his story was still taking up all the airtime. The reporters were still reiterating, "Ladies and gentlemen, this man is armed and very dangerous." But then an anchor chimed in, "We've learned that police are searching random houses in various neighborhoods. We will not disclose where the searches are taking place, so as to not hamper their investigative work." He also said a reporter from their station was now in Dallas interviewing some of Dean's family members.

"Turn it off," he said softly. That was followed by about twenty-five minutes of silence. I wanted to ask him to explain what really went down, but I decided not to.

"Go get that box so that you can make your phone call," he said as he approached me still sitting at the table.

While I was in my room I looked at the window and realized that since I was on the first floor, I could easily unlock it, squeeze myself out, with the box, and run. It would be a tight fit, but as long as my breasts and booty didn't have to go through together, I could do it. I tiptoed over to the window, looked out, and saw kids playing in the playground. I opened the window and was about to throw the box out when I remembered the look on his face when I offered him the deal. His smile seemed sincere when he was cooking for me. He looked frightened while listening to the news. He didn't scare me anymore. I wanted to keep my word to him.

I closed and locked the window and went back to the living room to find him sitting on the floor in front of the sofa. He had somehow found my Scrabble game and was setting it up on the coffee table. I handed him the box. He opened it and asked, "What's your mother's number?" I told him and he dialed it and put on the speaker. "Don't be long."

"Girl, you're gonna live long," Mom said. "I was just sitting here talking about you."

"Oh, yeah, who with?" I asked.

"Pat is here," she said. "We were just talking about the singles ministry at the church. They are planning some kind of ski trip with a bunch of other churches. I want you to go."

"I can't ski." I tried to cut her off. "How is Auntie Pat doing?"

"Patty's fine." She wasn't having it. "You don't have to know how to ski. It's about taking the trip with other single people so that you can find somebody."

"I'm fine being single," I said. I couldn't believe I was talking about skiing and boyfriends with a fugitive in my living room.

"You don't have to marry someone on the trip. It would be nice if you had a date every now and again," she said. "It makes me sad to see you showing up to all the family functions alone."

"That's how I like it for right now. I have a lot on my plate as it is." I rolled my eyes.

"Well, all I'm saying is that it would be nice to see you with someone." She went on to touch a nerve. "I'm sure Gary is looking down hoping you would move on. He's been dead for going on four years, Audra, you—"

"Wow," I interrupted. "Mom, my job is calling on the other line. I'll be busy most of the day so forgive me if I don't call back," I said.

"Yeah . . . okay," she said. "Love you."

"Love you too."

Dean hung up the phone and asked, "Anybody else you need to call?"

I thought for a minute, "Yeah, let me call my friend Casey." Once again he dialed the number.

"What's up?" she answered, sounding all groggy like I had just woken her up.

"Hey, were you still sleeping?" I asked.

She yawned. "Yeah, what time is it?"

"A little after noon. You must've gone out after we hung up!"

"Naw." She snickered. "Marcus brought his sexy ass over here, and when I say he fucked the shit out of me, I mean he fucked the living shit out of me until the sun came up." She then let out her signature I-had-sex scream and laughed.

"Wow." My eyes were opened to capacity. I was so embarrassed. "Ummm, so what are you doing today?"

"Him again, hopefully." She giggled. "I don't know. What's up? What are you doing?"

"I um, have some, ah . . ." I was stuttering. "I have some work I have to do."

"Okay. Did Darryl ever make it over there last night?" she asked.

"No," I lied, in an effort to keep the conversation short. "He didn't come."

"With his sorry ass," she complained. "There is a killer on the damn loose in your area and he couldn't even stay the night to make sure you were safe?"

"He did call, though." There I was taking up for him again.

"Whatever," she said. "I haven't watched the news yet today. Have they caught that guy?"

"Umm." I looked over at him. "I don't think so, at least not a few hours ago when I glanced at it on TV they hadn't."

"With his handsome self," Casey said. "He could get it."

"Ooookay." I tried to change the subject. "I guess I'll . . ."

"Oh, and oh, my God, this is such a small world," she said. "Guess who used to fuck with him."

"With who?" I was confused.

"The killer guy," she answered. "Guess who fucked him?"

Me? I didn't know if I wanted to hear what she had to say. He didn't look like he wanted to either. "Who?" I asked.

"Courtney," she said. "Rayna's sister."

I looked at him with a can't-you-do-better-than-that? face. "Courtney?" I asked to be sure.

"Yep!" Casey went on, "It turns out that dude is hung like a horse, heard he's great in bed and eats pussy like there is a famine."

"Oh, my God." I was uncomfortable for both of us. "All right, girl, my mom is calling me on the other line. I'll talk to you later."

"Okay. Tell her I said hi," Casey replied.

"Oh, and I'm turning off my phone to avoid hearing from or being tempted to talk to Darryl, so just leave me a message if you need me."

"Okay. Bye."

"Bye."

He turned off the phone. "I have no clue who Courtney is."

"Sure you don't," I joked.

"No, seriously," he said. "She's obviously talking about the wrong guy. Hung like a horse? C'mon." He laughed. "I don't have it like that, but I have enough."

"Yes you do." I couldn't believe I said that. "I didn't mean to say that."

"So it *wasn't* enough for you?" he asked boldly.

"Yes, it was." I blushed and repeated, *"Yes, it was."*

"Cool, 'cause I see that you have all of those Zane and Terry McMillan books in your office. I know that in those books men are always working with no less than a damn foot." He laughed. "I hope I didn't disappoint."

I was going to break out sweating soon. "There isn't a dis-appointed bone in my body."

"That's funny," he said as he placed the phone back in the box. "I didn't think I had any effect on your bones, just your irresistible tight and juicy flesh." I was floored. I couldn't fol-low up his comment with any words ever used in the English language. "How about a game of Scrabble?" he asked.

"That would be awesome," I answered.

We played the game for an hour or so before we hit a stale-mate. It happened when I spelled out the word "hyper" and he followed up by adding "bole" to the end of it.

"What's that?" I asked. "What is a hyper-bowl?"

He laughed, "It's pronounced hy-PER-buh-lee."

"What does it mean?" I panicked because it would make his sixty-point lead even larger.

"A hyperbole is a deliberate exaggeration," he said. "But go ahead and run it through your laptop as you have done for seventy-five percent of my words." He laughed again.

"If you insist." I was already connected to dictionary.com for cheating purposes. I entered "hyperbole," and sure enough it was a word. "Ugh!" I bit my bottom lip and looked over at him.

"Sorry to tell you, but that was a triple word score too. You wanna keep going? I can do this all day. I'm a literary disciple, baby!"

"Fine, I give up," I said very softly.

"What was that?" He pretended not to hear me. "You what?"

"Game over," I said loudly.

"Who won?" he asked jokingly and leaned over and tickled my arm. "Huh? Who won?"

"You!" I shouted.

He reached for my hand. "Good game." We shook on it.

"You mind if I check my e-mail?" I asked.

"Sure." He was still all smiles. "I'll have to watch you, though. Can't have you sending out smoke signals."

"Why would I?" It was another statement that came out of my mouth without thought.

"Why wouldn't you?" he asked.

I looked right into his intimidating eyes and said, "Because I gave you my word."

"Let's check your e-mail, then." During the game he had me use the computer while it was on the coffee table so he could see exactly what I was doing. I grabbed it and put it on my lap as he moved over to sit next to me. I had a bunch of forwards, jokes, and sale advertisements, nothing special.

"I'd love to check my e-mail," he said.

"Here." I handed him the laptop.

"Are you crazy?" he asked. "The minute I do that, SWAT will be outside. I'm sure they are watching everything I'm linked to."

"So why even worry about your e-mail, then?" I asked.

"I'm not so much worried about my e-mail. I'm worried about my daughter. Whenever she can't reach me on the phone she sends me e-mails." He paused. " 'Hi, Daddy. I love you, I miss you, and I can't wait to see you. I got an A in math.'" He smiled, shook his head, and continued. "That's my baby. I would love to hear from her right now."

"How old is she?" I asked.

"Seven."

"Wow." I exclaimed. "And what's her name?"

"Destiny," he said proudly. "Destiny LeAnn Tyson."

"Beautiful name."

"Thanks." He threw his head back on the couch and sighed heavily. "She might be blaming herself for what I did yesterday."

"Why would you think that?" I asked and then took the opportunity to find out what really occurred. "Tell me exactly what happened yesterday, Dean?"

JOURNAL ENTRY:

Dean

Her mother and I are no longer together," I said. "This would've been my weekend with her." He smiled. "I would've picked her up this morning. Tanisha, her mother, and I don't see eye to eye often, so I decided to call her to make sure that everything was still good and Destiny would be with me this weekend."

"Okay, I'm listening." Audra ushered me on, and from that point I relived the whole day as though it was happening again.

"Hi, Daddy!" Destiny answered the phone.

"Hey, sweetie!" I was shocked to hear her voice. I glanced at the clock, and just as I thought, it was a few minutes after eight. "What are you doing answering the phone? How come you're not at school?"

She hesitated. Of course she wasn't going to be quick about telling me that she was playing sick . . . again. "'Cause I was bleeding," she whispered into the receiver.

"What?" In my mind I immediately blamed Tanisha for whatever had gone down. "What happened? You fell?"

"No." She continued to speak low, almost as if she was telling me a secret. "I was bleeding from my pocketbook last night."

"What?" I was confused but laughed. "Destiny, how could your purse be bleeding? Be for real! Why aren't you in school?"

"My pocketbook, Daddy," she said shyly. "You know, my private girl part!"

Oh, my fucking goodness! "What did you say?" Dammit, I wasn't ready to deal with her having a period. Thank God I was done shaving because I would've nicked myself. I walked back into my bedroom and sat on the bed. Suddenly I wondered what in the hell these fast-food joints were really feeding our kids. Destiny is only seven years old and starting her period already? "Did Mommy talk to you about what that means?"

"No." She sighed. "After her and Hershel stopped fighting, she just told me to forget about it and not to tell anybody, especially you . . ." Her voice started to crack, and she was crying. "But it hurts, Daddy. I can't even walk right."

"Huh?" I knew nothing about cramps, tampons, and pads. "What does it feel like? Well, baby, you know I don't have . . ." I didn't know what to say.

"It's painful," she cried. I must admit that sometimes Destiny is more dramatic than Tanisha.

I tried to comfort her. "Your mom will give you something to make your tummy feel better."

"She told me to forget it, Daddy." She sounded scared. "She's mad at me!"

"Mad at you?" I was confused. "Why did she tell you to forget it? Where is your mom?"

"She's in the bathroom." By this time my baby girl was weeping. "Daddy, I didn't know that I wasn't supposed to do it . . . I was just doing what he said I *had* to do."

"What? Who? Who told you to do something?" My heart sped up as though it knew that I would need the extra blood pumping through my veins in five . . . four . . . three . . . two . . . one.

"Hershel." Her voice trembled. "A few weeks ago he started asking me to put his private in my mouth, so I did. And then a couple of days ago he asked if he could rub it on my pocketbook and I let him, but then last night when he did it it hurt more than any of the other times, and when he was finished I had white stuff and blood on me. So I told Mommy and now she's mad at him *and* me," she said. "But all I did was what he told me to do."

My heart, mind, and soul all broke into what seemed like twenty-five million tears. My mind went back to the day I watched all six pounds two ounces of her spring into the world. From that very moment my heart wrapped itself around her and my life was no longer my own. Every breath

I took was for Destiny, every penny I made was hers, every chick in my life, *since Tanisha*, had to learn to make chicken souse because that's what my baby wanted when she spent the weekends with me. But from the minute the doctor said, "It's a girl," I knew that on her wedding night I would be absolutely sick to my stomach thinking about some bastard being on top of my daughter. I couldn't handle this shit. My baby wasn't even eight and some grown ass . . . "What the fuck did you just say, Des?"

"Daddy, don't be mad at me, I—"

"I didn't mean to curse," I interrupted her. "I'm sorry! I'm not mad at you, baby, understand that . . ." Anger was dripping from my eyes and had my whole body stiffened up. "I'm mad, but not at you." I stood up but couldn't bring myself to take a step. I clenched my fists and nearly cracked the phone. I punched the air. I couldn't even say anything to her. "Give your mom the phone."

"She's in the bathroom, in the shower," she said.

I tried to be calm. "Did she take you to the hospital?"

"No, sir." She cried.

I didn't want to scare her, but I had to ask, "Did the police come by there?"

"No, sir."

"Put your mom on the phone," I demanded.

"She's showering," she whispered. "Plus, I wasn't supposed to tell you!"

I couldn't be polite anymore. "Go to the bathroom and give her ass the phone." I was finally able to lift one foot and then the other until I was close to the wall. My intention was to tap, not pound, on it until I heard Tanisha's voice, but two seconds in I was wiping chalky drywall dust from my knuckles.

"Mommy." I heard the sound of running water accompanying Destiny's whimpering voice. "Daddy wants to talk to you."

"He's here?" Tanisha sounded frightened.

"No, he's on the phone," Destiny said.

"Shit!" The water stopped and I heard the shower curtain pull. "Des?!" My guess is that she saw Destiny's tears. Tanisha tried to cover up the phone and asked, "Did you tell him?"

I heard my well-mannered little baby answer, "Yes, ma'am."

"Didn't I tell you to let me deal with this?" Tanisha asked her and continued to try to keep her voice down. "Go wake Hershel up. Tell him he's gonna be late for work." She turned her attention to me. "Hey, Dean!"

"What the fuck!" was my greeting to her. "You still got that fuckin' bitch-ass mutharfucka around my daughter?"

"First of all, good morning, and you don't even know half the story," she said. "Talk to me before you start running off of the handle like that."

"How in the hell can you still have that bastard in your apartment, Tanisha?" I asked. "Why haven't you called the police or taken her to the fuckin' hospital?"

"Are you going to let me talk or what?" she asked with an attitude.

"Talk." My head was spinning. "What the fuck happened?" My stomach felt funny. The breakfast I had couldn't be content with the pictures now running through my head. "Did that bastard touch Destiny? That's all I want to know."

"That bastard you're talking about is my husband now. We got married last week." Tanisha had the nerve to say that proudly. "Destiny just wants me to herself. She's spoiled."

"Did he touch my child?" I shouted at her.

"No," she yelled back. "Nothing like that happened, Dean. Relax."

"How do you know that nothing happened?" I asked. "Destiny said that he put his fuckin' dick in her mouth . . ."

"Hershel said he didn't do anything to her," she said. "You know Des ain't never liked him in the first place. She's just trying to break us up."

"So you're taking *his* word over your own daughter's?" I couldn't believe this simple bitch. "How in the fuck would she know that a dick goes into a mouth or inside of her? She is seven fuckin' years old. Where would she learn that bullshit?"

"I don't know. Maybe she saw something on the Internet." Tanisha dismissed it all.

"Internet my ass, Tanisha. Why would she be crying? What the fuck was the white stuff? And why in the fuck is my baby girl bleeding down there?" I took a deep breath. "That fat sorry-ass correctional officer wannabe bastard you have laying up in your bed is fucking around with my baby, and I will go to hell today to it see that he is dead." I hung up the phone and put on the jeans I had on the night before, a clean T-shirt, beige and black Timberland hoody, and my black boots.

I threw up my breakfast and cried like a baby over the toilet. I felt weak. I was physically ill and fast approaching mental instability. I thought about praying, but I figured God would make me do the right thing and I didn't want to.

My phone kept ringing, but it became background noise to me. I knew my life would never be the same again. In my hand was the lockbox, and though I hadn't opened it in more than a year, the combination was fresh in my mind, 8-2-7, my baby's birthday. In it lay my future—two Glock 19s and four loaded magazines. When Destiny was born, I whispered into her tiny ears that I would never let anyone hurt her. And now that someone already had, I felt like either I had to kill him or kill myself for not keeping my word. It was simple: he had to go.

I loaded a magazine into each handgun and pushed one into the waist of my jeans and hid the handle with my shirt. I put the other into the front kangaroo pocket of the sweatshirt. I grabbed Destiny's class photo from my nightstand and headed out to my car. Ms. Lopez, my next-door neighbor, said something to me, but I couldn't bother with her at that moment. Hal, the newspaper vendor on the corner, whom I bought a paper from every day, was tapping on my window and I couldn't even look his way. I was running lights, speeding, and just plain out driving in a tunnel of anger.

I entered the Florida Turnpike at Naranja, going about

eighty-five miles per hour, and less than two minutes down the road two state troopers were behind me with blue lights blaring. Full of rage, I took a deep breath as I stopped. I shook my head and said, "This isn't good."

The first officer asked for my license and registration, and I gave them to him with no problem. However, they both came to deliver the news that my license was suspended. I had no clue what they were talking about and I expressed that. When the first cop returned to his cruiser to check on something, the second cop said that my license was suspended because of two unpaid tickets.

"Two unpaid tickets?" I said and took another deep breath. When I first stopped the car, I worked hard on being calm and achieved it somewhat. While waiting on them to run my license I even convinced myself that instead of going to Tanisha's apartment to act a fool, I'd pick up Destiny and take her to the hospital and let the police get involved. I'd handle things the right way. "I don't have any tickets," I said to the cop.

"Well, what do you have?" Officer Friendly totally flipped the script. "What, all you have is the big dick you niggers walk around bragging about, huh?"

"What?" I was shocked.

"All you niggers want to do is fuck to spread AIDS or have fucked-up-looking kids." He cackled. "Keep spreading that shit around and maybe all of you will vanish and things could go back to being the way they're supposed to."

"What the fuck are you talking about?"

"You!" he yelled, with his hand now on his gun. "You

probably have AIDS and probably a kid or two, so you should do us all a favor. Go fuck your daughter, give her the virus, and kill two birds with one stone."

"Tell me you just didn't say that," I said. This Porky the Pig had just said the wrong thing to the wrong black man on the wrong day. How was I ever going to get help for Destiny if that was the level of respect the police were going to show me? "Tell me you didn't just say that shit."

"I said it, nigger!" His hand was still on his gun, "What you gonna do about it, boy?"

His words taunted me. This wasn't the '50s or '60s. This was 2009. "Fuck you," I said.

"No, fuck you!" He was angry. "Get your ass out of the fuckin' car right now," he shouted. He grabbed for the car door handle and hocked a wad of spit into my open window. I reached for my gun.

He couldn't get the door open so he reached for his gun, but mine was already in my hand. I knew that he was itching to shoot me—just another dead "nigger" who had pulled a gun on a cop. Then Destiny would be subjected to Hershel and his evil ways for the rest of her life.

The cop popped the button to his holster to free his gun and I felt that if he got to his gun first I was as good as dead. Destiny's face was all I wanted to see, so in rage and fear I squeezed the trigger, watched him fall, saw the other officer approaching, pointed the gun at him, and when I pulled back onto the highway two officers were down and I was officially on the run.

* * *

"I drove another couple of miles, left my car on the turnpike, ran into the mall, bought an outfit, saw a movie, and when night fell I was walking and hiding in the dark until I ran into you." Retelling the story now, it seemed like I had so many options, but at the time I felt I had no choice.

"Wow," she said. "I'm sorry, Dean, I'm a little speechless . . ."

"I hope now you realize that I'm not the deranged "Turnpike Killer" they're making me out to be." I paused and stumbled over my words a bit. "I just lost it for a minute, but apparently that was long enough to cost me my life."

"Dean . . ."

"I wasn't shooting to kill." I put my head in my hand. "I was just trying to get to Destiny. I was so pissed that I wasn't thinking. All I wanted was Hershel's bitch ass."

"I know, and I'm so sorry to hear about what happened to Destiny." She rubbed my back. I was shocked. Maybe she did believe I wasn't a monster.

"I don't want to talk about it anymore." I didn't want to think of Hershel another second. I quickly changed the topic. "I saw that you have some beer in the fridge. Let's crack a couple open."

"It's two in the afternoon," she reminded me.

"Yeah, but it's five o'clock somehwere," I joked.

She stood up and declared, "I'm not a beer drinker, but I'll get a couple for *you*."

"C'mon, I'm not about to drink alone." I followed her to the kitchen. "What *do* you drink?"

Audra gave me a glance. "I have a few bottles of wine that I can choose from."

"Choose one, then," I said as I opened the refrigerator and grabbed two beers. "Let me guess, these Michelob Ultras belong to your *boy*?"

"You know it," she said. "Drink 'em all. I couldn't care less."

"What's the deal with him, anyway?" I asked. "How come your mother doesn't know you have a boyfriend?"

She thought I didn't see her roll her eyes, but I did. "She's never met him."

"Why not? It sounds like it'll make her happy to see you with someone. Why don't you just take him around?"

"He has a girlfriend, if you must know," Audra answered. "So almost everything we do is behind closed doors or in places that *she* has no clue exists."

I would think that a woman like her would be through dealing with such bullshit. I frowned at her as I opened my first beer. "Why are you dating a man with a girlfriend?"

"I'm going to need a glass of wine to get into all of that." She chuckled. She selected a bottle of Riesling. "It's a long story."

"Let me get that for you." I grabbed the corkscrew as she passed me the bottle and took it and the beer into the living room. After opening it, I turned on the television. I quickly switched it to HBO and worked my way up to the other movie channels until I landed on *Superman Returns*. It was just coming on. Of course I had seen it nineteen times, but I couldn't get enough. I am one of the biggest Marvel comic book freaks you'll ever find.

"Cheers," she said as we brought together our glasses.

"Cheers." I smiled back and said as she touched my bottle with her glass, "Do you mind?" I pointed at the television.

"Not at all," she said and tried to whisper, "especially if it means that I don't have to tell you the story of Darryl anymore. What is this, anyway?"

"*Superman Returns.*" I spanked the couch with my hand. "Sit down. You're in for a treat."

She sat next to me, and by the end of the movie, which is nearly three hours long, she had about one swallow of wine left in the bottle and I had gone through about five beers.

"Now it's officially after five o'clock *here*, so you don't have to feel like a lush," I said to her. "Why don't you get another bottle? I'll help you drink it."

"Dean," she partially slurred, "I cannot possibly drink any more."

"You're putting me out in the morning." I grabbed her hand jokingly. "This is the least you can do for me . . . or with me."

"Oh, goodness," she said. "Fine." She got up and brought over another bottle.

I opened it and poured us each a glass. "So, tell me, what do you do?"

"What do you mean?" She looked at me strangely. "What do you mean what do I do?"

"What type of work do you do?" I asked.

"Oh." She giggled. "I'm in marketing and advertising. I

work for a company that creates online ads." She looked over at her laptop. "I actually told a client that I would put in some extra work for them this weekend."

"Well, I'm sorry I'm taking up so much of your time," I teased. "Maybe tomorrow you'll get some work done."

"Maybe!" she responded, blushing.

On the second glass of the new bottle she was laid out on the sofa and I was now on the love seat. The bottle of Riesling was the only thing that could hold itself up.

Audra was gorgeous. I looked at her, in awe, as though I had never touched her. All I could think about was kissing her. I didn't get to do that before. She was talking and I was studying her body like there would be a pop quiz.

Damn. She was talking, and I knew that at some point I'd have to break in with a "Huh?" but for now I was trying hard to dream up a way to see her naked again. I wanted to see her pussy up close and personal. I wanted to part her pink and brown meat and watch the juices flow and feel my fingers get slippery when she got wet. Something about her made me want to taste her pussy. And I knew she would appreciate it.

"So what would you have done?" she asked.

"Huh?" I finally let on that I wasn't listening. "Done about what?"

"Are you serious?" She giggled drunkenly. "I just told you that whole story."

"I'm sorry. I was just—"

"Looking at my legs." She playfully hiked her dress up from where it fell at her knees. "Can't keep your eyes off of me?"

"My hands either," I whispered.

"What did you say?"

"Nothing." I smiled. "Nothing at all."

We took our time on our third and final glasses and even played another quick and drunk game of Scrabble. Several of my words were made up and this time it didn't even matter to her. It was anything goes. She wasn't checking the computer or hassling me about pronunciation or spellings. She was having a good time.

Later that evening, I was embarrassed to call myself a chef—we ordered pizza. I was in no condition to cook. We destroyed that large pepperoni pizza and started winding down around ten o'clock. I think my common sense caught up with me while in the bathroom. Why? I was taking a shower with the door closed and she was on the other side of it. My freedom flashed before my eyes. I pretty much expected the police to be waiting with guns drawn when I opened up the door. So what did I do? I washed my hair with her Herbal Essence shampoo. If I was going down, I figured why not go down dandruff free, dammit.

This was probably how she planned to leave me, without a gun and a semi-erection to defend myself with. How did I become so vulnerable? I left the water running as I dried off. I listened for something that would imply other people being let in to the house. I didn't even hear her; she was probably across town already. "Shit," I whispered. I was scared to open the door. I wrapped the towel around my waist, grabbed the knob, gave it the ole here-goes-nothing turn and pulled it toward me. I stepped out and amazingly nothing happened. I walked into her bedroom, and she was passed out on the bed.

"Audra." I nudged her. "Audra."

She moved a little. "Huh?"

I said, "I left the water on for you. You asked me to."

"You did, baby?" she slurred. "You gonna get in with me?"

I shot her an I-hope-you're-serious look. "You want me to?"

"Come on." She stumbled to her feet. "I need you to do my back."

I was more than excited. "I can do that."

"You know I like when you stand behind me in the shower, Darryl." She flirted and touched my chest. "I love when you bend me over, Daddy."

Wow! That knocked the wind out of my sail. She wasn't *really* talking to me. She thought she was talking to that dude . . . and she was calling him Daddy. "Audra." I grabbed her hand and called her name loudly to make her look into my face, and when she did I said, "Go ahead and get into the shower."

"Oh, goodness." She looked a tad embarrassed when she realized that it was me and not that Darryl guy. "I'm so sorry." She walked into the bathroom as I laughed it off.

I needed a pair of relax-fit shorts or something to walk around in and to possibly sleep in, so I went into the drawer I'd seen her get some male clothing from earlier. When I saw the purple silk bag all zipped up there was nothing that screamed, *Open me*. However, there was a little whisper coming from it. It said, *Don't you wanna see what's inside?* So when my fingers touched the zip, I realized that I had hit the jackpot. The bag was filled with sex toys, sensual lotions, massage oils, and other gadgets. My first instinct was to put it back quickly, but then I had a better idea.

JOURNAL ENTRY:

Audra

I opened the bathroom door and found the entire house in darkness except for my room. Dean had found my candles and seemed to have each and every one lit. "What's this?" I asked calmly.

He was naked and approached me slowly. "I wanted to set the mood for the show," he said.

I was trying hard not to look at his dick. "What show?" I asked.

"The show that you're going to put on for me." From behind his back he revealed what I had nicknamed my purple pussy bag, not only because it was purple but also because that probably was the color my pussy looked after I had used all the items in the bag. He placed it in my hand and said, "I'd love to watch you." He opened my towel and I let it drop to the floor. "I won't touch you. I just want to watch."

"Are you serious?"

"Very serious." He whispered into my ear, "I want to see you use everything in that bag." He walked me over to the bed. "Do whatever you do when you're here alone."

"Okay." I sobered up tremendously as I crawled onto the bed. Looking at his sculpted naked body had me wet already. "Tell me what you want me to do first."

"Do whatever you would normally do." He tried to be nice about it, but I didn't want him to.

"No, you tell me." I threw the bag in his direction. "This is your show."

He grinned and fished through the bag and pulled out a bottle of strawberry shortcake edible lotion and passed it to me. I sparingly applied some to my fingers and massaged the cream into my breasts, paying extra attention to my nipples, pulling and pinching them. My breasts were large enough for me to push them up and lick and suck on my nipples a bit. I stared into his face the entire time, and when my eyes dropped below he didn't have to tell me that he liked what I was doing—his dick did.

Next he handed me my silver bullet. I knew that I was about to act a fool because it had new batteries in it. I turned it on and placed the silver egg on my clit. Initially, it was slip sliding all over my pussy because I was so wet, but I finally found my spot, and my eyes automatically closed. It felt so good, I started moaning loudly. I moved the bullet back and forth between clit and my lips.

I envisioned both Dean and Darryl in the room watching me. Darryl wouldn't be able to watch for very long. He would've had his dick in my mouth ten minutes ago. I loved sucking on Darryl, and I could only imagine how that would feel while Dean tongued my pussy lips. The fantasy was so overwhelming, my pussy cried juicy tears of pleasure. My body was heaving and humping air. Dean's thick hand was gripping and slowly moving back and forth over his meat. I felt like coming again.

I reached for the purple bag and grabbed my dildo. It was my turn to watch him. I rubbed the faux dick head between my wet lips and continued on down. I enjoyed the way the veins protruded from it and felt on my skin. Dean knelt between my legs, still stroking himself, bringing his show closer to me, and as I moved to slide my dildo into me he grabbed my hand and said, "As long as I'm here you don't need to put anything fake inside you." He moved his face toward mine and I could now feel his car pulling up to my garage. He hit the button and I slid up and opened to him . . . but he didn't park inside. He drove into me, reversed, drove in but reversed again. "I'm sorry," he said. "I should've asked you first."

"No." I was already panting. "Give it to me."

"I have no problem giving you this dick." His voice trembled as he slid into me again. "You don't have to use any of those toys while I'm here. Your man should be embarrassed that you need all of that shit. He's not doing something right." My insides feel like liquid silk. "Damn, you feel so fuckin' good," he whispered.

He was right. All of those gadgets were to keep me occupied when Darryl wasn't around. "Oh, yes," I cried as his fleshy hard meat hit a spot that no dildo or vibrator could ever touch. "Oooooh."

"You like that?" he asked.

"I love that."

He hit that same spot again and again until I felt like I would black out. The way I was screaming, I wouldn't be surprised if the police broke down the door. It sounded like a domestic violence case. *Yes, officer, he's beating me, arrest him for manslaughter, he's killing this pussy.*

I could hardly speak. "Oh, God!" I ground my body and all of its liquid on him. "Fuck me, baby."

He didn't stop handing me that dick for a second. "So you call him Daddy, huh?" he asked.

My eyes rolled back. "Oooh, baby, that's good." I tried to ignore his question.

"Oh, you can't hear me?" he asked half joking and proceeded to put both my feet on his shoulders. "Maybe this will open up your ears."

The next time he pushed into me I fell into "falsetto" and was singing just like The-Dream. "Ooh ooh baby, aah aah aah aah." In a high-pitched voice, "oooh my . . . oooh shit."

"Who's your daddy now?" he asked. Dean was working hard, and with the next thrust there was a new ruler to reign over all of the lands within me. "Who's your daddy?" he asked again.

"You!" I yelled with passion. "You are."

"Say it," he demanded as he continually stumped my pussy. "Say that shit."

"You're my daddy," I cried. "Fuck me, Big Daddy. Tear it up."

He flipped me onto my side, put one of my legs up in the air, and used his dick to control every sensation I had for the next twenty minutes. He bullied my pussy, didn't let it breathe, he held it down and kept beating it. I loved it. "I'm coming." I couldn't not say it, it was too powerful. "I'm coming, Daddy."

"Come on, girl," he said. "Come on this dick, let me feel it. Put it all over my dick." I came so hard that I probably would've squirted if he wasn't inside of me. I didn't realize that I was screaming until the room got quiet and I noticed Dean groaning loudly. He released into me and yelled, "Damn." He panted heavily. We both collapsed onto the bed and stared up at the ceiling.

Dean pulled me close to him and I draped my arm over his chest. He was rubbing my arm, then my back, and he fell asleep.

It was about six in the morning when I woke up and found myself sprawled out in bed. I realized I had too much space—Dean was gone. The sun wasn't up yet, so I turned on the light. "Dean?" I called out. I walked through the apartment and he wasn't there.

"Damn," I said and plopped down on the sofa. I couldn't notify the police and say that he had been here. Was I supposed to act like it was all a dream and forget about it? Could I be arrested for harboring a fugitive? Or go to jail for not escaping when I could? Probably.

My heart was conflicted. He had left without saying goodbye. I didn't want to be sad, but I was. I should have been glad he was gone. I told him that he had to leave first thing in the morning. I just didn't expect to be so worried about him. "Turn yourself in," I said softly, hoping that my words would somehow find their way to his ear. I could already see myself writing long letters to him in prison. "God, please protect him," I said.

I reminisced on the couch and made up my mind that I wasn't telling anyone about Dean. I wasn't spilling the beans to a single soul.

Suddenly Dean emerged fully dressed from the bathroom. "Good morning." He smiled. "You're up early."

"What?" I was stunned. "I thought you were gone. Where were you? What are you doing?" How many questions could I ask without taking a breath?

"Sorry," he apologized. "I'm about to head out now."

"Why were you in the dark?" I asked.

"I needed to think," he said. "Getting my thoughts together." He looked frustrated and like he had been crying.

"Are you all right?"

"I'm cool. I better get going before the sun comes up."

My heart sank into my chest a little. I would miss him. I didn't want to turn on the TV later to hear he had gotten shot or killed by the police. I was close to tears. I didn't want to look desperate.

"Thank you so much for allowing me to stay," he said as he walked toward me with his hand extended.

I opened my mouth but my vocal cords were connected to my ass. "Do you need money?" I barely asked.

"Money?" He looked away with the sexiest smile I had ever seen. "I could never take money from you."

"Dean, I really want you to be all right," I said candidly.

"Money is the least of my problems," he said.

"Do you want to take my car?" I asked.

"No." He was thrown. "I don't want to involve you in this any more than I have already."

By now the tears had leaked out and I just looked plain insane. "Just take it, mail me the key, and the address where you left it." I tried wiping my eyes before he could see what was going on, but it was too late.

His hand touched my face. "I'm not taking anything from you, Audra. You've given me enough." He smiled. "All I ask is that you keep me and Destiny in your prayers. Okay?"

"Okay," I promised as he pulled me into an embrace and lined my forehead with soft kisses. "Please take my car," I begged him. Had he been a hardened criminal I wouldn't be worried, but Dean was a good man. He had just made a mistake. He wasn't a bad guy, and now he was scared and I was scared for him. I hugged him and cried. "I don't want anything bad to happen to you. I want you to get as far away as you possibly can."

He just kissed me. He pressed his lips hard onto mine a few times. Our tongues snuck pass our lips and connected.

There had to be a nerve ending that ran from the mouth directly to the clitoris because, no lie, my lower lips and clit felt the effect of our kiss as though they were being sucked on. He backed me up against the wall and slightly pulled away. "I've been thinking about kissing you from the second hour of knowing you," he said.

"Me too," I confessed.

"*Now* there is only one thing left to do," he said as he untied my robe. "I can't leave without tasting you." He pulled the robe from my body and cupped my pussy with his hand. He rubbed and teased it as our lips joyfully strangled one another again. Before long he lowered my body to the floor, stretched my legs apart as far as the hallway would allow, and teased my clit with his tongue. He had a smooth technique: sensual licking in small circles, soft nibbling, fairly aggressive yet tantalizing suction, and using his fingers to part the lips to pierce his tongue in and out of the depths of my pleasure while fingering me. He ate pussy like there was a famine and he would never eat one again. I encouraged him, "Don't stop." He devoured my juices as though they were dripping from a porterhouse steak.

All hell broke loose within me when he placed my clit between his lips and pulled so hard that I thought he would walk away with it. He let it snap back into place and went after it again. He did that four times before my vagina had a monologue. "I don't want you to go." It was my pussy talking, but it came out of my mouth. "Stay . . . You can stay until tomorrow." I was breathing heavily. "Don't go." This time the words came from my heart.

"Dean," I groaned, "you make me feel too good." I gave in 110 percent to what I was feeling and felt my body squirt out the liquid consequences of my actions. The remainder of it trickled down my lips to my ass and I lay paralyzed for at least a minute. My eyes were closed and I panted and panted until my breathing regulated, and even then I found it hard to move a muscle.

When I opened my eyes and my senses returned to me, he was standing over me with his hand outstretched to help me up. "Thanks," I said, holding on to him until I was on my feet. "That was amazing." I smiled.

"Was it?" he asked.

"Yes it was, indeed."

"I'm glad I'm leaving you with a smile."

"Leaving?" I wanted to ask. I just told him that he could stay.

"You don't want to stay?" It rolled off my tongue like drool. What in the hell was my mouth trying to do to me?

"Huh?" He was dumbfounded.

"Nothing."

"Naw." He smiled. "What did you say?"

I sighed. "I was asking if you wanted to stay." I tried to make myself believe that I was just being nice. "I mean you don't have to, I was just—"

"Do you *want* me to stay?"

"It's not all about you staying." I tried to clean it up as I tied my robe and brushed past him to get to the bathroom. "I just don't want anything to happen to you," I said in the most fake and nonchalant voice I could dig up.

He followed me to the bathroom. "Would you like it if I stayed?" he asked again.

"Yes." The word jumped out. I was a little embarrassed, but that feeling was less than the emotions I knew I would have if I heard about the "Turnpike Killer" being shot dead in a hail of bullets by Miami-Dade PD. "Yes, I would like you to stay so that we can figure out what you should do."

"Thank you." He grabbed my hands. "But I don't want to get you deeper into this."

I smiled up at his unbelievably handsome face. "I want you to stay so that we can at least try to figure out a way for you to see Destiny before anything goes down." I squeezed his hands a little. "That's the least I can do for you."

"Naw, that's the *most* you can do for me." He kissed my forehead. "Thank you."

We went back to bed, this time with the purpose of sleeping. We both woke up hungry but there was hardly anything in the house to eat. "I'm gonna run to the store," I told him.

"You don't have to," he quickly responded.

I shrugged. "Publix is right up the street."

"You can't go," he said.

"You still think I'm going to run?" I said. "I'm the one who asked you to stay."

"No, it's not that." He looked troubled.

"Then what is it?"

"Once you leave here and come back," he said, "that's where shit hits the fan. You would've been given the opportunity to turn me in and since you didn't, that could put you in jail."

"But no one knows that," I said.

"True, not right now, but if the police ever found that out . . . I'm sure they have cameras in there. I don't want you in this bullshit. I'd rather them think that I was holding you against your will."

I saw his point. "What about if I go to the Farm Store? I won't even have to get out of the car."

"It's not about going to one store or another," he said. "I don't think you should leave here at all."

"What about me going to work tomorrow? I have to. I have a major client depending on me."

"I'll get out of here tomorrow, then," he said.

I took a deep breath. "Okay."

He stared into the refrigerator. "You have bread and some cheese. That could only mean one thing." He laughed, "Grilled-cheese sandwiches."

"Sounds good to me." I giggled.

JOURNAL ENTRY:

Dean

Ready?" Audra asked as she stepped into the kitchen wearing hip-hugging jeans and a red shirt.

"Yeah," I said, removing the last sandwich from the skillet. "I'm ready for you." I placed the grilled-cheese sandwiches on two plates.

"Thank you, chef," she joked as she took her plate.

"Nothing chef about it. You could've made them better." He laughed. "I didn't do anything special."

"Just having a man cooking in my kitchen *is* special," she said. "Shoot, having anyone other than me cooking in the kitchen is special."

I sat down and decided to get to know her. "So, pick one of the three—your age, your weight, or your social security number."

"Huh?" she asked. "For what?"

"Pick one," I said.

She thought for a minute. "My age . . . I guess."

"What is it?" I asked.

"Thirty-two." She grimaced. "I usually tell people twenty-twelve, though."

I laughed. "That's cute."

"It's cute now, but on my thirtieth birthday you wouldn't have wanted to be within a mile of me." She bit into her sandwich. "I was pissed."

"Why?" I was glad to turn thirty. "You actually don't look a day over twenty-five or six."

"Aw, Dean, what are you trying to do?" She smiled big.

"Speaking the truth, that's all." I had another question already waiting. "So how come you don't have any children?"

"Children are something I am not sure I want yet." She was honest. "But I'm not getting any younger, so I guess I need to decide pretty soon."

"You've never met a man who wanted to have kids?" he asked.

"Well," she said and let out a single chuckle, "I *was* engaged to be married, so I guess it would've eventually led to kids."

"Why didn't you get married?" I wanted to know more.

"He died," she said vaguely.

"Whoa, I'm sorry." I wasn't prepared for that. "May I ask what happened?"

"A car crash, four years ago." She didn't seem to want to expound on it.

Then I remembered something her mom said on the phone. "Is that the guy that your mom was referring to?"

"Yep, Gary."

"I'm so sorry to hear that." I wanted to know more but didn't want to press her. However, she started talking on her own.

"Our wedding was five months away," she said. "The accident happened while he was on the way back from the post office. He had just mailed off all of the invitations, all one hundred and sixteen of them." She put down the sandwich and stared over at the other room. "The day of his funeral was supposed to be my first fitting for my gown, that *same* Saturday." Any sign of a smile was now miles away.

"We don't have to talk about it if you don't want to."

"I don't mind talking about it." She looked at me and tried to smile. "I don't think there will ever be another man to walk the face of this earth like Gary. No one will *ever* love me the way he did. It's like God played this nasty trick on me, made me think that my life was going somewhere and just pulled the rug from under me, ya know?"

I knew that she needed me to say that I did.

"For about two years I completely shut down," she continued. "I went to work and that was it. But then I gradually started opening up again, started dating here and there, only to end up in the shitty situation I'm in right now with Darryl." She rolled her eyes. "Gary is probably turning over in his grave about the way Darryl treats me."

"Why are you with him, then?" I asked.

She hesitated. "I love him."

"Does he love you?"

She didn't look at me when she answered. "He says he does."

"Does he act like he loves you?"

"Sometimes he does and sometimes he doesn't. Most of the time, it's about him and his girlfriend."

"What do you mean?" I was glad she was opening up.

"He calls her several times a day to say hi, to check on her, or to let her know where he is, and even though he's lying to her, I would love it if he called me like that. Instead, he sends me text messages. He calls once a week, and most of the time he's just returning my call."

"Are you serious?" I laughed but it wasn't funny. I just thought it was funny that it's true that the jerks get the best women. "And this is the guy you're crazy about?" I asked her.

"Yep." She looked up at the ceiling. "He says he will leave her to be with me, but I think that if he were forced to make a choice he'd probably stay with her, even though he claims that he can't live without me. I know those are just words; his actions show something totally different."

She was frustrated, but I had to tell her the truth anyway. "You wanna know what I think?" I asked, though it wasn't a question. "He's playing you. You can't be *that* stupid!"

"Excuse me?" Audra turned her neck toward me, hood-style.

"A man knows within the first few minutes of meeting a woman how far he wants her to go in his life. So though he may like you and enjoy having sex with you, his girlfriend is the one he can't see his life without, because if he loved you he'd do anything to be with you."

"You're probably right," she whispered.

"Oh, there is no probably in it."

"When we first met he complained about all the problems they were having." She snickered. "But surprisingly throughout all these months things have gotten better between them. Now he says he's in love with her." She smiled, but I could hear her heart crumbling. "He says he's in love with us both."

"Damn, he's really got you going."

She seemed embarrassed. "I guess."

I couldn't hold my tongue. "He's an asshole if he doesn't want to be with *you*."

"So why am I the one who feels like the asshole?" Her voice trembled.

"You shouldn't. This guy is no good . . . don't let him drag you down," I said. "You need to get out of the relationship or you'll be one of those bitter women who treat a good man like shit just because of what this guy is doing to you. Don't let it go there."

"I know." She seemed defeated.

"Okay, there has to be something good about him," I said. "What is the last gift he got you?"

"He's never given me a gift," she said.

"Valentine's Day?" I asked.

"Nothing." She grimaced. "I prayed that every floral arrangement that came through the door at work was for me, but I got nothing." She seemed ashamed. "I didn't even see him. He spent that evening with *her*, cooked a romantic dinner for *her*."

"Did you get him something?" I asked.

A tear fell from her eye. "I don't want to talk about it. It just makes me feel more and more stupid when I think of how I've put myself out there for this man."

"What about for your birthday?" I asked. "What did he give you?"

"Amazingly, God decided to play another trick on me. She and I have the same birthday." More tears fell. "He promised that he'd spend it with me. I made dinner reservations at my favorite restaurant, got a hotel room on the beach, and that morning he called and told me he couldn't make it. He didn't want to lose her."

"You need to let him go. If you were my sister, my daughter, my cousin I would say the same thing: he's playing you."

She sighed heavily, then the room fell silent for several minutes as we finally ate. Then she took the opportunity to change the subject. "You always wanted kids?"

"Hell, no. I actually always said that I never wanted kids."

"Why?"

"Well, freedom. I didn't want to be tied down to anyone or anything. I didn't want responsibilities, blah, blah, blah." I took a deep breath. "But it was really because of how I grew up. My dad left when I was very young. I grew up feeling incomplete because I didn't have a father." I paused. "So when it came to thinking about having kids, I felt there was no way I could know how to be a father without ever having had an adequate example of one." I smiled. "But Destiny came along and proved me wrong. I am her father, and in her eyes I couldn't be any better."

"Good for you," she said.

I had a warm feeling when I looked at Audra. "I wish we had met under different circumstances."

"Why is that?" she asked.

"Because I would love to blow this Darryl character out of the water by showing you what a real man is supposed to be like and how you're supposed to be treated."

I was lying on the floor thumbing through *The Art of Seduction*, which she had on one of her bookshelves.

The book was very interesting, to say the least, and I was wondering if she had tried any of the techniques on anyone . . . including me. So as night fell and her work was winding down, she made more and more time for chitchat and I posed the question. "What form of seduction do you find works best?"

"Come here and let me show you." She pushed back from her desk a bit.

"Yes, ma'am." I hopped to my feet and made my way over to her.

"Right here." She beckoned me to sit on the edge of the desk. She then rolled the chair closer, looked up at me with those full sultry eyes, and said, "I've never read that book." She untied the strings of my sweatpants. "But how about you let me know how seductive this is." She lowered my pants to midthigh and lifted my shirt to reveal an already hardened penis. Still looking up at me, she trailed her lips with her tongue, leaving them spit shiny, and gave the head of my dick a soft peck.

Soon that innocent peck turned into her tongue encircling the tip of my rock. "This is all I've been thinking about doing since I first sat down here," Audra said.

With a chuckle I confessed, "That's funny, because this is all I've been thinking about since you sat here too."

Audra giggled and continued. She had already licked me up real good and I was ready for a good sucking. I prayed to God that she could suck dick because the Lord knew that I was past due for some good head.

Finally, she parted her lips and moved them over my piece. I was so anxious that my hand flew to the back of her head before I even knew if she had skills, but oh my goodness did I find out quickly. She folded her lips over her teeth and brought her mouth down onto me, sucking me in like oxygen. "G'damn, Audra." She was good. She applied just the right amount of saliva, suction, and sexiness to the job. She worked her hand up and down the shaft that her mouth hadn't reached. Her rhythm was perfect. I closed my eyes and the warmth and snugness of her mouth reminded me of her tight, hot pussy, and I had to work hard to contain myself.

Okay, Lord, she can suck dick. Thank you! She was definitely good enough to bump Trina from the number-eight spot of my top ten 'head-bangers' list. Thank God she wasn't looking down at my curled-up toes, because she'd know that I was at her beck and call for the moment. The more she sucked on my stick, the farther up the list she moved. She backed up and slowly came down on it, taking it in all the way down to the shaft. "Oooh, damn!" I felt myself softly tapping into her tonsil. Wow, she had just kicked Yolanda out of the number-four ranking. She started taking me in faster and deeper, and before long she booted Kim from the number-three position. I was shocked. My top three had been in place for more than seven years; nobody had ever touched them. I didn't believe that she could get any farther up the ladder, though—there was only one way to earn number one or two.

She kept pulling me into her wetness and looking straight into my eyes as she did it. She was so sexy. I wanted to kiss her, but I couldn't stand the thought of taking my dick out of her mouth. "Oooh, that's good shit, baby." She teased me with her tongue some more and sucked down the sides of it all while softly moaning. She groaned as she started sucking me down to the shaft again. "Suck it, girl." Oh, she did.

"Do me in the mouth, Dean," she said.

I asked, "Do what?"

"Do it," she said shyly. "Do me in it."

Her statement shocked me, but she didn't have to repeat herself. I stood all the way to my feet and slowly started to penetrate her orally. She was still applying suction, and the feeling was incredible. I began moving a little faster and she didn't seem to mind. I then gently placed my hands behind her head to keep her where I wanted her and started plunging into her mouth as I would've her pussy, and she took it. I felt no teeth, nothing but spit, tongue, cheek, tonsil, and suction.

I felt my load moving to the hilltop of my dick and warned her, "I'm about to burst." She didn't budge, and that turned me on even more. "It's coming, baby," I announced, and she didn't get out of the way. She was about to earn herself second place on my list. "Oooooooh." I came in her mouth (she was now number two), but wait . . . she was still sucking my dick, which meant she swallowed. *Ding ding ding*, ladies and gentlemen, the winner and *new* champion. Audra had knocked Dana out and was now reigning number one on my 'headbangers' list—she swallowed.

"Damn, girl." She was still sucking me, my joint was still hard. "Turn around, bend over, and let me get in that sweet pussy." I lifted her dress and sank into her wet lips from the back as she hugged the office chair.

"Oh, yes, Dean, get it," she moaned. "Get it!"

"I'm getting it, baby." I held her around the waist. "Fuck me back."

I got what I asked for. She started moving that ass of hers and almost made me come again in about a minute, but I held out and gave her another six or seven minutes before I shot another load. We took a shower together, got in bed, and worked up *yet* another sweat.

JOURNAL ENTRY:

Audra

"So," I started speaking and hoped that I wasn't giving him puppy dog eyes, "you have my number, right?"

"Yeah." He wrapped his arms around my waist and took a deep breath.

"One way or another I'll call you tonight," he promised and lowered himself to me until our lips touched. He kissed me as Alicia Keys suggested, "like you'll never see me again."

"I can't believe I'm about to say this, but I think I'm going to miss you being here," I confessed.

He laughed and said, "I think I'm going to miss being around here."

I didn't want to let go, but he had a Greyhound bus to catch at 4:05 and it was already a little after three in the morning. Earlier, online, I bought him a ticket to Seattle, but he would probably hop off long before he reached the

Emerald City. I bought it using Darryl's name and gave him Darryl's driver's license; he had misplaced it months ago and had since gotten another.

Dean refused my offer to drive him to the station. It was going to take him thirty minutes to get there on foot. "Be safe," I said as I smiled up at him.

"I will." He let go of me and reached for the doorknob. I wanted to cry. "Be smart," he said, touching my cheek, "and no more being Darryl's number two."

"Okay!" I promised, playfully putting my hand over my heart.

"I mean that," he said. "You're a good woman and you deserve more than that."

I blushed. "Thank you!"

He smiled as he opened the door, and in a flash Dean and all our time together was just a memory. I fought the urge to jump into my car, pick him up, and bring him back to my place, my room, my bed, my pussy but more important my heart. When the clock read 4:05, my heart sighed. It would miss having a *real* man around. I lay in bed, but there was no way that I would fall asleep with such memories in my head.

I wanted to call Casey and tell her about my weekend. I wanted finally to brag about amazing sex with someone with a damn heart and a brain. I picked up the phone, but what would I say his name is? Where did I meet him? Why would *she* never meet him? Dammit, I had to keep my secret. At six I got up and got ready for work and was out the door by seven fifteen.

* * *

"Wow," Jennifer said as she approached my workstation with her coffee mug in hand. "Somebody's glowing." She smiled. "You must've had a fabulous weekend."

"I did," I answered. "It was awesome."

"Tell me all about it." She sipped her coffee. "What did you do?"

"Nothing much, actually." I wanted to blush. "I stayed in the house the entire time."

"Wow." She gawked. "I used to love those types of weekends," she said, then added, "but with kids that never happens."

"You have to make some time for yourself, Jen. Let Ralph take the kids out on a Saturday and you just sit at home and do nothing." As the comment left my mouth I knew I was wrong. There was no way that Ralph, her boyfriend, was going to volunteer any of his free time to spend with her rude-ass children. Jen had three kids, by three different men, and she had been married three times. You'd think her tubes would be tied in a knot, stapled, and safety-pinned for safe-keeping, but no, she used babies to keep her men interested. After she suspected Ralph of cheating, now she was actively trying to get pregnant and hoped he'd be husband number four. Poor Ralph didn't know about her ovulation kits, early morning temperature charting, and invisible birth control. So, like most men, free blow jobs and pussy got in the way of his good judgment. He should've seen the signs, but he was about to fall for one of the oldest tricks in the book.

"Wait! Oh, my goodness." Jennifer looked astonished. "Wasn't that whole killing thing in your area?"

I looked at my computer screen and tried to change the subject. "Oh, I saw that ad you did for that construction company—nice work."

"You know that guy is still out there, right?"

"Yeah, they still haven't gotten him," I said.

"Aren't you scared?" She was bugging out.

"Scared of what?" I kept checking my e-mail.

"The guy, Audra," she continued. "He shot those cops, so I'm sure he'd kill me . . . or . . . you if he had to."

"I'm concerned, but I'm not scared," I replied. "He is probably long gone by now."

"But where in God's name could he be?" she pondered. "They had the streets shut down just minutes after everything happened. They had helicopters in the sky. It's like he just disappeared," she said. "I live miles and miles away, but I was looking over my shoulder all weekend. I'm sure he wouldn't think twice about raping me."

Yes, he would, I wanted to say, but I instead said, "You're absolutely right." Please, Dean wouldn't touch her with triple-layer latex gloves on. "Is there more coffee left in the pot?" I asked her.

"Jeff isn't here yet, so there should be." She laughed. "I'll check." She walked away and yelled back from around the corner, "Yeah, half a pot."

"Thank you," I shouted back and picked up the phone to call a few potential clients. I was glad that most of them didn't answer. With so much on my mind, leaving a voice mail was much easier. Throughout the morning I kept checking the local television stations' websites in hopes of not seeing that he had been dragged off the bus, beaten and arrested, or shot to death.

Going to work was a bad idea. I don't know how my paranoid ass ever thought I could act normal and make it through an entire day. I was so extremely nervous that by noon I almost had no fingernails left, and when my cell phone rang, I think I peed on myself. The call was private, and on any other day I would've sent it to voice mail, but I took a chance and answered. "Hello."

"Hey." His voice made my body and mind quiver. "I wanted you to know that I'm all right."

"Good," I said, then nervously picked up a pen to doodle. "I was hoping you wouldn't forget me."

"There is a lot on my mind, a lot that I need to be figuring out." He sighed. "But instead of thinking about those things I can't stop thinking of you."

"Really?" I blushed. "Me?"

"Yes," he said, "and often."

"How often?" I flirted.

"About as often as a dolphin has to surface for air," he said and quickly followed with, "I gotta go, bye."

"Wait," I said, but I don't think he heard me say it. I didn't even get to ask him where he was.

I immediately Googled dolphins. I learned that because they don't have nostrils, dolphins surface every fifteen to

twenty seconds to clear their blowholes with a burst of air.
"Aw," I cooed at the information. I was thinking about him
every fifteen to twenty seconds too.

I was happy to hear from him, but that lasted about five
minutes before I realized what I had voluntarily involved myself in. I was giddy over a man who had committed murder. I
had myself a cop killer and was helping him get out of town. I
became afraid that I would never hear from him again. I would
be sitting in prison while he sipped on margaritas in Tijuana.

Each time the elevator doors opened I was ready to put my
hands up and surrender. I was expecting FBI agents to storm
through the office and haul me away. I knew I needed to take
the rest of the day off when I received an e-mail from my
boss with the subject line, *Do you know Dean Tyson?* My heart
jumped. What did he know and how did he know it? I didn't
want to open it. I'd rather just walk off of the job, not quit or
resign, just disappear.

I sat in a paralyzed state for a minute or two; I truly
couldn't bring my body to move. I just continued to stare at
the computer screen until I found the courage to open the
e-mail. In it Spencer rambled on about how one of the officers
killed was his wife's brother-in-law's sister's friend's uncle or
something, but no real relative, and he was seeking vigilante
justice. He had copied and pasted a picture of Dean into
the body of the e-mail and had typed "Do you know Dean
Tyson?" across the bottom. I wanted to reply, "Hey, buddy, get
off of that porn site and open up your office door so that the
cleaning lady won't walk in on you squirting come all over

your hands and licking it off again you damn freak." Instead I just deleted it.

I pretended to work the rest of the day. I couldn't focus or shake the cloud above me, so I left fifteen minutes early. By five o'clock I was already on the train making it to my car when my phone rang. It was the exclusive Darryl ring tone, "*No one, no one, no one . . .*" Several people on the train looked at me with the aren't-you-too-grown-to-have-a-musical-ring-tone? stare.

Without a greeting, Darryl spit out, "What time will you be home?"

"Why?" I snapped.

"'Cause I'm coming to get my things," he said.

"Your things?" I wanted to laugh. "You don't have that much stuff at my place."

"I have a whole drawer full of stuff," he said. "It might not be much, but it's mine."

I agreed that he could come get his measly boxers and shirts.

"If your dude will be there, then just put my shit in a bag by the door 'cause—"

"He won't be there," I interrupted.

"Who in the fuck is he, anyway?" Darryl asked. "Where the hell did this guy just appear from?"

"Why?" Suddenly the tables had turned. "Is that the real purpose for your call?"

"No. I want my shit," he whined. "But I'm entitled to ask who in the hell that dude was or is . . ." he paused. "Because I thought it was you and me—"

"No, you couldn't have thought that." I struggled to keep my voice down. "You couldn't think that 'cause it's been me, you, and Jasmine for the damn longest time. It's never been just me and you."

"Whatever." He brushed me off. "There you go with that shit."

"What shit, Darryl?"

"If she's not around to talk for herself, then don't bring her up."

"Bring her around, then," I said. "I'll talk to her. I have a lot to say to her."

"She's not the one fuckin' around on me," he said. "This is between you and me."

"Nothing has ever been just between us. She is always in the middle of every fuckin' thing we do."

"Don't get brand-new. You knew about her when we first met," he said. "I never lied to you. I'm not about to deal with you and the dude. So I'm getting my shit out of your place and I'm bouncing, simple."

"So what's good for the goose isn't good for the gander, huh?" I asked.

"Fuck the goose *and* the gander," he said angrily. "I'm not laying up with a woman who is laid up with everybody else."

I had run out of patience. "I've been an option for you for far too long. Kiss my ass, and because more than half of the shit you have at my place was paid for with *my* money, don't bring your ass there." I hung up.

An elderly woman on the train was staring at me in

disdain. I felt like shouting. If she uttered one word to me I was going to let her have it too. She stood up as the train neared the approaching station and looked down on me with eyes overflowing with sensibility and wisdom. Her mouth slowly opened. "Don't you take any bullshit from these trifling-ass men." I was floored. She continued, "tell that bastard where to go and just how to get there, but don't you go there with him." She winked at me and made her way to the door.

I smiled at her. "Thank you," I said.

I had stopped by Publix to get a few bags of groceries and lo and behold, when I got home, Darryl walked up to my car with an empty duffel bag. I paid him no mind. I opened the door, entered, and tried to slam it in his face, but he stopped it with his hand. Darryl threw himself down on the sofa like a disgruntled teenager. "Where've you been?" he asked.

"It's none of your business."

"I've been waiting on you. We need to talk." He tried to be polite.

"We don't need to talk," I informed him. "You know where your things are."

"Oh, it's like that?" He stood up.

My blood was still smoldering. "You do not come into *my* place and think that you're in control. No, that's not about to go down. You can get the things that I bought for you and leave."

He walked up to me and tried to hold me around the waist. "No hug?"

"Hug?" I pushed him off. "Let you tell it, I'm screwing everybody and their granddaddies too. Why would you want to touch me? I may have the bug!"

"I'm sorry, babe," he said. "It's just that that shit hurt! I came here to be with you and a mufucka with no shirt comes to the door talking shit." He shook his head. "I felt like a fool."

"Well, welcome to the club. I've been the president of the fools' society for about eight months. I'm a damn fool every g'damn night, knowing that you're with her," I said. "So man up and deal with it."

"Deal with it, hell!" He shook his head. "Because of my situation I'll let you have that one time, but no more. You get rid of him." He glared at me sternly. "You got that?"

"No I don't 'got that,'" I said. "I'm not standing in line for you anymore, Darryl. Tell Jasmine's insecure, immature ass to stop calling my private number to see if our background noises are the same. Tell her that you are all hers now. I don't care if you tell her in English or Spanish, but you tell her that shit and tell her I said it." I smiled. "I don't want your slimy conniving black ass for one more second."

I had never spoken to him in that manner, so he looked shocked. Normally, in this time frame, his dick would have already pleasurably punctured several of the holes in my body.

"Have it your way," he said.

"It's about damn time."

He brushed past me and marched down the hall with his

duffel bag. I went into the kitchen, put away my groceries, and poured myself a glass of wine. I sat on the sofa awaiting his triumphant return. He was in my room for about five minutes, and then I heard him in the bathroom, no doubt gathering his razor, toothbrush, and contact lens case and solution. "I'm missing some boxers and a couple of pants and shirts."

"Yeah, I know," I answered.

He was frustrated. "Where are they?"

"Dirty," I said. "I'll wash 'em and have 'em FedEx'd overnight so that you won't have to come back."

"Ha-ha. Why is my shit dirty, Audra?"

"How do things get dirty?" I asked jokingly.

"How did *my* things get dirty?" He was curious.

"Because my guy needed something to put on." I purposely delivered the straw to break the camel's back. Darryl was in front of me in no time. He snatched me to my feet and got right in my face.

He spewed, "If I so much as dream that you actually let some funky-ass nigga wear my shit, I will hurt you." I must've really pushed a button. Darryl was a lot of bad things, but he wasn't violent, especially toward women.

"I think you'd better go," I said as I walked over to the door and opened it.

"You putting me out?" he asked with a slight grin. "So this mufucka means that much to you that quickly, huh?"

"No," I corrected him, "I mean that much to myself—that quickly."

"Whatever!" He walked out.

Honestly, my heart nearly walked out after him. I never in a million years thought that I would open my door and invite him to walk out of my life without running after him. Up until that moment I felt like I couldn't go on without him in my life. But look at me—I was breathing just like every other day of my life. It had been only minutes, but I was living without Darryl.

I rolled around in my ultrafeminine strength for all of ten minutes before I broke down in tears, wineglass in hand, on the sofa. I fell into what Oprah calls the "ugly cry," you know, when your bottom lip curls under, you can hardly open your eyes, and your tears form waterslides down your face. You just look plain ugly. I called Darryl dreadful things starting with each letter of the alphabet. I was on R for retard when there was a knock on the door. Wow, maybe Darryl did have a soul after all. I got up and thought about wiping my face but decided against it. I wanted him to see the pain and anguish he had caused.

I unlocked the door, opened it about an inch wide, and walked to the kitchen and poured more Moscato into my glass. If he wanted to come in, he knew what to do. I heard him reluctantly enter and wanted to shout, "Oh, don't act like you didn't just knock on the damn door to come back in."

"Hello?" Then he asked softly, "Where are you?"

I didn't answer him. I just took a swig of my wine and leaned up against the counter. I closed my eyes and heard him making his way through the living room, and by this time I knew that he had to have spotted me in the kitchen. I wanted him just to say he's sorry or that I was right. Instead, I felt him softly kissing the areas of my face that were saturated with tears.

"I couldn't leave," he said.

"Why not?"

He wrapped his arms tightly around me. "I couldn't get on the bus."

"Huh?" I opened my eyes and stared into Dean's eyes. "Oh, my goodness . . ." I didn't want him to know that I thought he was Darryl. "What happened?" I asked as I embraced him. "I thought you were out of state by now."

"Well, I should be as far away from Florida as humanly possible," he said. "But the more I thought about being so far from Destiny, the more steps I took away from the bus." He shook his head. "And the more I thought of you and how you've been so good to me, a stranger, a fugitive at that, the more I wanted to be wherever you were." He tightened his hold on me. "So here I am."

I was speechless for several reasons. Though I was happy and flattered that he was back, I was concerned about being smack-dab in the middle of this illegal drama again. However, there were strong arms holding me upright now, and for the moment that was more important than anything else.

"Why are you crying?"

"Am I crying?" I asked sarcastically and tried wiping away my tears.

"What happened?" he asked. "I saw him come and I watched him leave."

I was astonished. "Where were you?"

"In that broken-down truck that's been parked out there for days," he said. "Been in it almost all day."

"Have you had anything to eat?" I tried to divert attention from what he wanted to know. "You hungry?"

"Why was he here and why are you crying?"

"I think it's really over this time."

"You should've wanted it to be over a long time ago, so why are you crying?" he asked.

"I don't know." And I truly didn't. "I was fine at first, and then I realized what my life is going to be like without him."

"What, you mean like full of meaning?" he asked mockingly. "Are you scared of being number one to somebody?"

"I'm not scared." I thought about it. "I want that, but what's the point?"

"What do you mean?"

"He'll just die and leave me all alone again." The past was now in the present. Funny, I had never connected the two before, never thought one had to do with the other, but I was learning quickly. "Of course it'd be nice to have that, but it stops at the grave. That shit can happen at anytime, so why even bother looking for Mr. Perfect?"

"That's the problem. You're looking for Mr. Perfect instead of Mr. Perfect *for You*." Dean stared intently at me but backed away from me at the same time. "Everybody has to die, so get over it," he said. "Don't use that as an excuse to settle for bullshit."

"All right, Dr. Phil. Would you like a glass of wine?"

"No. But I would love to feel your pretty brown lips on mine."

"Which ones?" I asked, batting my eyelashes at him.

"Let's start with the ones I can see right now. I'll work my way down to the others."

That's all he needed to say.

JOURNAL ENTRY:

Dean

God knows that I tried to leave. I wanted to get on that bus, but something wouldn't let me and I felt like I made the right choice. First on my mind was Destiny. Leaving Miami meant leaving her behind, and even though I couldn't see her I was satisfied with breathing air that possibly passed her smile . . . hoping to get a hint of her innocent fragrance in the air. I couldn't do it. Also, leaving behind the only friend I felt I had right then would be devastating. Though Audra was still somewhat of a stranger to me, I had essentially trusted her with my life. However, coming back to her wasn't an easy decision. I regretted putting her back into the middle of my ordeal, but I had nowhere else to turn.

After her lips left mine, I asked playfully, "So did you tell your coworkers all about our weekend together?"

She replied, "Oh, yeah, I told them all about you." We both laughed. "So what is the plan now, Dean?"

I guess that was her way of telling me that I couldn't stay there forever, and I was fully aware of that, but I didn't have a plan. I couldn't leave without seeing my daughter, because I didn't know when I'd see her again. "I don't know . . ." I was more than just confused. "I truly don't know."

"Well, you have to come up with something," she said.

It wasn't her fault that I was in this situation. "I know I can't stay here forever, and I'm sorry to get you involved in this again."

"I know," she said. "I just want you to be okay, and I'm scared that sticking around Miami is only going to mean trouble for you."

"I feel the same way, but I have to see my baby again and make sure she is all right before I just up and leave."

"Do you think that calling Tanisha and coming up with a way for that to happen can work?"

"No. I'm sure they're listening to all of her calls," I said. "And if they're not, they're probably following her every-where, so I can't take the chance."

"True," she answered and continued to think. "What if we went to her school and just watched her from a distance?"

"I want to talk to her," I said. "I need her to know that I'm okay and even though she won't see me for a while that I love her and will think about her every day." Just the thought of her not being a short car ride away was freaking me out inside. "I have to talk to her."

"Okay." She tried to soothe me by rubbing my head. "We'll think of something, but for now let's just talk." She smiled at me.

"Is that all you want to do?" I asked.

She blushed. "No, but I'm trying to remain respectful of the type of day I'm sure you've had."

"Forget about my day." I gawked at her. "Disrespect me."

"I can be very disrespectful." She flirted as she sat on my lap facing me.

"Be rude, baby." I brought my lips to hers once more. "Let the bad girl out to play."

A few minutes later she was on her knees disrespecting me and everything that I stood for. Boy, did she disrespect me, and I returned the favor randomly throughout the night ... tenfold.

She contemplated staying home from work the next morning, but I encouraged her to go. I assured her that I wasn't interested in trying on any of her clothing, shoes, and/or makeup—she could trust me to be there alone.

When she left I kept the blinds closed and sprawled out on the bed watching the news. Thankfully, the media had turned away from me because three armed men robbed a bank. They cleaned it out and killed seven people when the security guard tried to be James Bond. They all got away, so the hunt was now on for them, and I was on the back burner. For now.

So three Hispanic guys were now scrambling through the city. I hoped they avoided capture, because the longer their faces were out there the sooner people would forget about mine. I'm sorry that people had to die in both instances, but their mistakes worked to my benefit.

I have a nervous habit that I had been trying hard to sup-
press for days, but since I was all alone I might as well just let
it go. Before I knew it I was in her bathroom with the Lysol
spray and a sponge cleaning. That's right. I will clean the hell
out of something, anything, when I'm angry, nervous, or anxious. Since I was two of the three, Audra probably won't have
to clean again for a few weeks. I scrubbed every inch of both
bathrooms, mopped, cleaned the mirrors, everything. Then I
vacuumed and straightened up the other rooms. The kitchen
was spic-and-span, and when there was nothing left to do I
started preparing dinner. I found an electric fondue pot in
one of the cabinets and decided that I'd treat her to something
special when she returned home. She deserved it.

JOURNAL ENTRY:

Audra

This would be the first time since being with Gary that I was coming home to a man. I was excited about having someone waiting for me and it wasn't just because he couldn't leave the house. I knew he wanted to be there. When I opened the door, I was stunned by what I call the clean-house smell.

Dean greeted me with a warm hug and a sensual kiss. He took my laptop bag and purse and set them aside, then handed me a glass of wine and ushered me to the bathroom, which was clean and filled with the smell of coconut and sound of running water and soft jazz. "Thank you," I said when I noticed the bubble bath. "Oh, my goodness." No one had ever been so thoughtful. He turned off the lights and the two candles on the counter kicked into overdrive to light the small room. "This is beautiful," I said as I looked around.

Dean undressed me and helped me into the tub. "Relax."

He smiled. "I'll come back periodically to check on you and then I'll do your back." He winked at me. "Dinner will be served whenever you decide you've had enough." He handed me my glass again and left the room.

I could just melt and slide down the drain, I felt so good. I was up to my nipples in milky white warm coconut water and bubbles. It was so sexy. I felt like a million dollars.

Later he washed my back. After about forty-five minutes of feeling like Miles Davis's spirit was in the room, I put on my silk robe and asked him through the door, "May I come out?"

"All right, mademoiselle, right this way." He offered his hand and a cheesy French accent. He led me through the dark house to the dining room table set for two, adorned with candles and a fondue pot. It was so beautiful! He pulled out my chair and I noticed a cute little menu he created. He called the restaurant Dolphin's Domain. The appetizer was a mixture of four Mexican cheeses with cubed Cuban bread for dipping. The entrée was rice pilaf, steamed broccoli, beef, chicken, and shrimp, and the dessert was listed as "me." I was speechless.

The jazz was still going and the wine was ever flowing. We spent most of the time flirting with each other. Suddenly, my phone rang. It was my mom. I hadn't spoken to her since a few days ago when I rushed her off the phone, and I knew she was probably salty. "I need to take this, okay?"

"Sure," he said, continuing to eat.

"Hi, Mama," I said.

She immediately asked, "Why haven't I heard from you?"

"Mama, we talked on Saturday," I reminded her. "It's Monday."

"Where are you?" she asked.

"Home," I replied matter-of-factly.

"Good," she said. "I'm pulling up right now."

"What?" My eyes nearly split at the seams. "What do you mean?"

"I just left the mall and I have to pee something terrible. You know how I am about public restrooms."

I stuttered in shock, "So *where* are you?"

"Parking next to your car," she said joyfully. "Open the door. It feels like I'm about to burst."

"Right now, Mama?" I asked, panicky.

"Yeah," she demanded, "open the door."

"Okay." I hung up and glared over at Dean. "My mother is outside."

"Wow, that's interesting. Has she been watching the news?"

"I'm sure she has," I replied. "So how about you hang out in my room for a while."

"No problem." He stood up and grabbed his wineglass. "How are you going to explain all of this?" He pointed at the table.

"I don't know." I smiled. "I'll think of something."

Though I knew she was coming, the knock on the door still startled me. "See you later," Dean said and disappeared.

"Lock the bedroom door," I whispered loud enough for him to hear me. "I'm coming," I called innocently to my waiting mother.

I turned on a couple lights, and when I heard him close the door I adjusted my robe and opened the front door. "Hi, Mama."

"Hey." She hugged me quickly, kissed me on the cheek, and said, "I gotta get to the bathroom." She threw down her purse and sprinted down the hall. I was right behind her.

"Shit," I said to myself as I saw the water in the tub and the candles still lit.

"What?" She looked back at me as she went to close the door. "You need to watch me or something?"

I laughed. "No, I just wanted to be sure that there was toilet paper in here."

She looked around. "There is, excuse me." With that said she closed the door.

Minutes later when the door opened she wasted no time with the comments. "Candles, bubble bath, jazz . . . wow!"

"Wow what?" I asked.

"Trying to unwind?" she asked innocently.

"Yeah. There's a lot going on at the office," I lied.

"Like what?"

"Like stuff you wouldn't understand even if I told you." I smiled. "Come on." I beckoned her down the hall to get her away from my bedroom, which she seemed drawn to.

"Wait. I want some of that mango lotion I had last time." She turned the knob, to no avail. "That stuff smelled so good." She tried again. Nothing. "Is this door locked, or is something wrong with it?"

"It's locked," I answered shyly.

Either she didn't have a clue or she was trying to play it smart. She said, "Open the door and let me get some of that lotion."

"No, Mama. It's locked, I want it locked."

She glared suspiciously at me. "Why?"

I started walking back down the hall, hoping she'd join me. "Let's talk out here."

"Ooooh." She finally caught on. "Well, excuse me," she said and followed me down the hall and made a nosey beeline for the table. "Mmmm," she gasped, "very nice romantic little setup! I guess I interrupted a special evening."

I smiled. "It's just fondue."

"Fon-who?" She giggled. "Y'all kids these days are too high-tech for me."

"It's where you cook your food right in the pot on the table," I said.

"That's too much work." She shook her head. "Why not just cook it on the stove?"

"It allows for conversation, Mama," I replied.

"Well, I don't talk when I eat and I don't eat when I talk." We both laughed. "So should I just hang around until he gets dressed?" My heart nearly stopped.

"No." He *is* dressed."

She smiled. "Great. Bring him out and let me see him."

"No, Mama, not today. I asked him to go into the bedroom because I'm not ready to introduce him to anyone yet."

She huffed. "You asked a grown man to hide from your mama?"

"He's not hiding," I lied. "He just respects my wishes."

"Audra." She sounded disappointed. "It's not right for you to have him caged up in your room like some wild animal." She scolded me. "What's wrong with him that you don't you want folks to meet him?"

Because he's the damn Turnpike Killer, I wanted to scream. "I do want you to meet him, but not today," I said. "I'm entitled to that, am I not?"

She snatched up her purse. "Do what you like." She was upset. "Talk to you later."

I grabbed her by the hand. "Mama, don't be mad," I said. "It's just that I don't know him all that well yet. I like him, but I want to get to know him and see that he's worthy of bringing around, that's all."

"I just want you to be happy, and I want to be happy for you." She smiled. "It's not about seeing you get married or even having kids. I just want my daughter to find happiness."

"I will, Mama."

"And when you do," she preached, "don't let nothing, not even me, get in the way of it."

"I will." I loved this woman. "Thank you, Mama." I hugged her. "Call me when you get home."

"Will do." She opened the door and then looked back at me. "He'd better be hot."

"I wouldn't have it any other way," I teased. "I love you!"

"Love you too."

When she pulled away I knocked on the bedroom door. "You can come out now."

He opened the door slowly. "Everything okay?"

"Yeah." I chuckled. "She wanted to meet you."

"Wow. Why didn't you come and get me?"

I laughed. "Come on, let's finish dinner."

Within a few minutes we were back right where we left off, almost as though there had been no interruption. Getting to know more about him was exciting. Oddly enough, I was falling for him. I knew that when he tried to leave again, it would be hard on both of us.

At the end of the evening I ended up on the sofa as he cleared the table and washed the dishes. He refused to let me help, and I wasn't about to ask more than once. The wine and jazz had me drifting on a melody and put me fast asleep.

I don't know just how long I slept, but it was certainly a pleasure to wake up with Dean's tongue a half inch into my pussy. "Oooooh," I moaned. He was awesome. He had mastered the flickering tongue or "boxing bag" technique and needed to host a workshop on it. I was sick of running into grown men who ate pussy like they still had a locker, detentions, and algebra homework.

My back arched up from the sofa and I couldn't help grinding my wet juices into his mouth. "Lick it, baby," I said, then groaned uncontrollably. "I need to feel your dick."

"Do you?" He stopped sucking on me long enough to ask, "You want it?"

"Yes!"

He stood up and quickly pulled down his pants. "How do you want it?" His dick was rock solid and his pounding veins were protruding. I grabbed it and kissed the tip innocently, and then I gave it a sloppy wet kiss. I licked and suckled the head and then slowly downed the rest of him—over and over again. I've been told that I'm a savage beast with my mouth. My skills are ferocious, so after about three minutes I could tell he wanted to come, but I needed that rod rammed into me. He'd have to wait.

We changed positions. He sat on the sofa and I stood in front of him. I dropped my robe and took a seat on his lap facing away from him with my feet on the floor. I rose up and slowly slid back down onto him. Each time I slid down, my wetness increased and the feeling intensified. He had one hand on my waist and the other massaging my clit. I was in pure ecstasy and started riding him so fast you'd think I was the jockey of the Kentucky Derby's winning horse. When he yelled out incoherently and I felt him burst within me, I wanted to shout out, "first place."

Dean panted. "Damn." He slapped my thigh. "Damn, baby." He was still breathing heavily.

My thighs and calves were on fire. It felt like I had just run the Boston Marathon. I had overdone it, and now my legs were quivering and hot. I was too embarrassed to try to get up. It felt like I would fall flat on my butt or, worse, my face. He must've been clairvoyant, because he picked me up and carried me to the bedroom as though he had read my lazy mind. Being a gentleman, he once again brought a warm towel and cleaned me thoroughly.

JOURNAL ENTRY:

Audra left for work and I was drained. There was no way I was pulling a Mr. Clean today. I was up at five in the morning thinking about Destiny, but I couldn't bring myself to get out of bed until noon. I wondered if Destiny knew anything about what had happened to me. Every plan I had to see her was foiled. I would have surely gotten caught. And even if I could get to her, I couldn't be sure that Tanisha wouldn't turn me in. There was nothing I could think of that made much sense.

I sat around most of the day thinking about my situation and wishing I could at least call my mother. I could use her advice. I knew that she was sick to her stomach worried about me. "Damn!" I wouldn't wish this on my worst enemy. I was disconnected from the entire world. One phone call to someone could take away my freedom.

I won't lie, though, there were several instances where

Audra's home phone and I had a staredown. I wanted to pick it up to hear Destiny's voice, but the police would be at the door within minutes after tracing the call. I noticed it was after four o'clock and Audra hadn't called as she had promised.

Six then seven o'clock came and she didn't call or come home. I tried calling her several times but my calls went straight to her voice mail. By ten o'clock I was panicking. Where could she be? I couldn't call the police; that would land us both in deep shit. I called the few hospitals to see if she had been in an accident, but she wasn't listed as a patient anywhere.

At midnight my mind was made up—she was more than likely in police custody. Somehow they had tracked me down and got to her. But why hadn't they come for me? Either way, I got dressed and was ready to surrender. I wanted to run, but something stopped me. I couldn't let her go down alone for this. She had done too much for me to run and leave her. I decided to wait and see what would happen. As the captain of all of this bullshit, I needed to go down with my ship.

I sat up all night. The sun came up and still there was no sign of her. I hadn't known her long, but I knew this was extremely out of character. If something bad had happened to Audra, I was worried that when it was learned that she and I had been together it would be concluded that I had something to do with it. I had to get out of there.

I touched the Bible on her nightstand and said a prayer for her, asking God to please watch over her wherever she was. I didn't know where I was going, but I had to get the hell out of her place.

The phone rang. I ran to the caller ID, it read "Florida Cellular" and a local 786 number. I didn't have her cell number memorized, but I knew it started with area code 786. I picked up. "Hello?"

There was silence and then a hesitant, "Hello?"

"Yes," I answered.

"I can hardly hear you. Who is this?" the female asked.

"Who is *this*?" I asked back.

"Umm, I'm sorry." She sounded confused. "Did I dial the wrong number? Is this Audra's number?"

"Yes," I said. "Who's calling?"

"This is Casey," she said. "Is she there?"

"No, she's not," I answered. "I was wondering—"

"I can just barely hear you," Casey interrupted me. Then she asked, "Is this Darryl?"

"Aaah." I didn't know what to say. "Yeah."

"Oh, okay," she said. "Is she still at the hospital?"

"Hospital?" I asked.

"When I left the hospital it was after midnight, and she was still there."

"She never came home. I've been waiting on her all night. What happened?"

"I thought you knew." Her tone changed.

"Knew what?" I asked.

"Mrs. Doris was in a very bad car accident night before last," Casey went on. "Apparently she had just left Audra's place and was taking the back road home. She was hit head-on by somebody in an SUV."

"Shit," I said, assuming that Mrs. Doris was Audra's mother. "Oh, man!"

"Yeah, Audra didn't even know about it until yesterday morning while she was at work," she said. "She's taking it very hard. She had asked her mom to call her when she got home, and she didn't remember to check on her when she didn't call."

"Which hospital?" I asked.

"Christ Regional," she informed me. "They don't think she'll make it, though."

I felt for Audra. "What's the room number?"

"She's in ICU and Audra has no phone reception, so if you want to reach her you'll have to go up there."

"Okay." I sighed. "Thanks."

"No problem," she said. "You have a cold or something?"

I assumed she was comparing my voice to Darryl's. "Yeah, I'm trying to shake it."

"Well, you didn't get it from me *this* time." Casey giggled. "Ummm . . ." She cleared her throat. "I must admit, I've been missing your late-night drop-ins." She paused, no doubt pondering if this was the appropriate time to say what she was about to say. "I promise I'm over that shit. I won't threaten to tell her again. I was drunk and I'm sorry," she said. "How about I come over there right now?" I was stunned; this was Audra's best friend. When I failed to respond, she asked, "Cat got your tongue? I have another cat that wants that tongue!"

"I'm going to the hospital," I said.

"All right, babe," she said with sex in her voice. "Call me later."

"Yeah," I said and hung up the phone.

I couldn't believe what I had just heard. Audra needed someone *real* at her side. "Damn!" She was there, beyond logic, when I needed her, so I had to do the same for her—beyond logic.

I looked around her apartment for something I could use to alter my appearance in some way. I found some reading glasses and a few unisex hats. Anything else would make me look like a raging homosexual. I laughed at my appearance in the mirror. The hat had her company's logo on it, but it was huge. Everybody who worked there must have craniums like E.T. It wasn't much of a disguise, but I damn sure didn't look like myself, and I knew she needed me.

I caught two buses and then walked for twenty minutes to get to the hospital. I used Darryl's ID to get a pass to ICU from the security guard. I made my way up to the sixth floor and showed the nurses the pass. They had to scan something on it and then informed me that only two people are allowed in the room at a time and I'd have to wait in the waiting room until one of them returned.

I made my way to the waiting room and sat down. The only other person in the room was an older white gentleman. He was watching *Family Feud* and didn't bother looking over at me. I removed the silly glasses but kept on the gigantic hat.

About ten minutes went by before a tall, skinny older man with red eyes walked in. He gave the room a few glances before coming out and asking, "Are you the one here to see Doris?"

"Yes, sir." I stood. "I'm a friend of Audra's."

"I'm Herbert, Audra's father." He extended his hand.

"Nice to meet you, sir." I shook his hand. "I am so sorry about what happened."

"Thank you." He took a deep breath. "This has certainly been quite a trying day," he said. "C'mon, let me walk you down there to the door, but only one of us can go in." He encouraged me, "You go and try to keep her strong, because right now I'm just as weak as she is."

"I'll try my hardest, sir."

We walked about twenty yards to a door numbered 611 and suddenly I realized what I was doing. I was bringing my drama into her real-life family tragedy and saying, "Deal with it." What if she didn't want me here? What if she had made up her mind that she never wanted to see me again? Who was I to push myself and my problems onto her during this sensitive time? "Go ahead in," her dad said.

"Okay," I said but still not really knowing what to do.

He didn't give me much choice because he pushed open the door and walked away. Audra turned around and looked right into my face. "Dean!" She didn't move and I didn't know what that meant, but I walked toward her, and before I was in touching distance she was reaching out for me.

"I'm so sorry," I said as my arms encased her. I rubbed her

back and kissed the top of her head. "I'm here for you," I said over and over again and just held her. I could tell she needed my strength, because she could barely hold herself up. "I'm here, sweetheart."

After several minutes of her holding me and sobbing, I looked over at her mom and it broke my heart. Her entire head was bandaged and several tubes were protruding from her mouth and neck. Her face was swollen and badly scratched. Several machines were beeping and humming around her. I thought about my own mother. She could also be lying in a hospital bed. I would never know because I couldn't call. I held Audra even tighter.

"I wanted to go outside to call you, but I don't have reception here." She cried. "But I couldn't leave her here, not even for a second. I'm scared of what might happen if I walk away."

"Don't worry about it," I said, kissing her.

"She never made it home that night," she said, "and I forgot to call and check on her."

"This is not your fault, Audra," I whispered to her.

"But I didn't check on her," she said.

"I know. But if you had called, she wouldn't have answered. You wouldn't have been able to do anything," I reassured her. "This is not your fault."

"How did you know?" she asked.

"Casey called to see if you were at the house, and I answered hoping it was you," I said. "I was up all night worried about you."

"I'm sorry, I—"

"You don't have to explain anything."

She took a deep breath. "I don't know what I would've done without Casey yesterday," she said. "She was here with me the entire day." She moved closer to her mother's bedside and continued holding my hand. "Mama, this is the guy I've been telling you about," she said. "He's the one who was in the room that night." She looked at me with a tearful smile. "His name is Dean." She squeezed my hand. "I know that I said I wasn't ready for you to meet him yet, but he wasn't having it and came anyway." She was crying again. "I told you he was hot."

I stayed there with her until three more people arrived to sit with the family. "I'll give you time with your family, so that they can come in and be with her."

"You'll be in the waiting room?" she asked weakly.

I pulled her toward me and spoke softly into her ear just in case her mother could make sense of what I was saying. "I don't think I should. There's a television in there and anything could pop up at anytime. I'll find somewhere to go and I'll come back in a couple of hours to check up on you again." I kissed her on the cheek. "Be strong, baby."

"I'll try," she said. "Don't wait too long to come back."

"Okay," I said, letting go of her.

When I went back into the hallway toward the waiting room, her father was surrounded by four or five people. They were all praying. As I walked toward the nurses' station to the elevator, I heard them talking about how no one has ever come to visit the patient in 652. Hmmm. I followed the

numbering and entered room 652. The old man, Henry Mat-
teson it said on his chart, had a private room and was sound
asleep. I plopped down in the chair by the window. My intentions were to flip through some channels and deem myself a
friend of the family if anyone walked in, but it was as though
some hypnotist had a swinging watch in front of me, saying,
"You are getting sleepy, sleepy, sleepy." I fell asleep.

JOURNAL ENTRY:

Audra

"Mama." I knew that if she could hear me, she would answer, but I kept calling out to her anyway, in hopes that something within her would fight to reply to me. "Mama."

Though I had been staring at her for hours, part of me still felt like I was in the wrong room. She didn't look like herself. She hadn't been wearing her seat belt and went through the windshield of her car. But although the woman in the bed didn't look like my mother, the warm and loving spirit she always walked around with was there, so I knew it was her.

The room door opened again. "How you doing, baby?" Auntie Pat asked as she walked in.

"I'm fine." I had a habit of saying that even on the worst days. Mama always used to tell me to stop lying.

"Now, I know you're not doing fine," she said as she hugged me. "It's okay, though, baby."

Patricia Berry and my mother have sat in the same pew at

church for more than twenty years. Passing each other gum, mints, and notes, and sharing offering when the other didn't have any, they were the best of friends. Seventeen years ago, when I was fifteen, Ms. Patty's husband died suddenly and left her and the three kids with next to nothing. They had to live with us for almost a year, which is when I started calling her Auntie Pat.

"Why don't you go home and get some rest, shower, and change," Auntie Pat said as she ended our embrace.

I had been sitting here with Mama for twenty-four hours straight with no sleep, but I said, "I can't leave her, Auntie Pat. I'm scared."

"Scared of what?" she asked.

"Of coming back and her being . . . gone." I was crying again. "I'm okay."

"No, you're not," she said. "You need to get some rest, Audra, plus these are the clothes you wore to work yesterday. You need to freshen up, honey."

I thought about it. Mama would kill me if she knew I was all up on her and hadn't washed between my thighs since yesterday morning. "Okay," I conceded, "I'll go, but I'm not going to sleep. I'll just shower and come right back."

"That's fine," she said.

"I'll see you when I get back, if you're still here."

"Still here?" she asked, as though I was insulting her. "Where else I got to be? This is my sister."

I kissed her on the cheek and then turned to Mama. "I'm leaving for a few hours, Mama, just so that I can change. I'll be right back." I touched her hand. "I love you." It still took me a few minutes to physically leave the room. I longed to be in her presence.

I went into the waiting room to thank everyone there for their support. My dad was remarkable. Though he and Mom divorced when I was eighteen, he was there like they had never missed a beat together. "Oh, Audra, the young man told me to tell you that he has a family member in room six fifty-two he is visiting."

I found Dean in room 652, still wearing that ridiculous hat. He was asleep while an older man was sitting up in bed staring at him. "Hi," I said to him.

"Hi." He looked confused. "Is that my nephew?" He must've thought I was a nurse.

"Umm, I'm not sure." I didn't know what to say. "Let me wake him up."

I walked over and shook Dean's leg. "Hey."

His eyes popped open. "Hey."

"Umm." I looked out of the corner of my eyes to signal to him that the man, whoever he was, was watching him. "Your *uncle* is up."

"Oh." His eyes widened, and then he smiled and faced the man. "Uncle Henry," he greeted the man. "I thought you were never going to wake up," Dean said.

"I've been up for a while." The man sounded heavily drugged.

Dean stood and walked over to Henry and gave him a big hug. "How are you feeling?"

"Well, I'm hanging in there," he said. "By the grace of God."

"Good, good." Dean looked at me with a smile and asked, "What's up?"

I tried to keep my voice down. "I'm going home to shower, grab a bite, and then I'm coming back."

"Okay," he said. "You ready now?"

"Yeah," I replied.

He turned to the man. "All right, Unc. I've been here almost all day waiting for you to get up until I fell asleep myself." He chuckled. "I have to go to work now, so I'll have to get going."

"Aw." The man was genuinely disappointed. "When are you coming back?"

"In a couple of days," Dean answered. "You keep feeling better until then."

"All right," Henry said. "Thanks for coming in spite of everything that is going on, and tell your mother that I'm sorry."

"I will." He hugged him again. "See you later, Unc."

Dean put on those glasses and we exited the room. "Do you really know that man?"

"Nope." He laughed. "I just needed a place to wait for you away from everyone else."

"Wow," I said. "You sure had me fooled."

"Him too," Dean said.

As we left the hospital I felt disconnected from Mama, almost like what I assume babies feel when the umbilical cord is cut. Well, my cord had been severed and now I had to breathe, but there was no air. Something wasn't right, and when we pulled out of the parking garage I was sobbing. I contemplated begging Dean to turn around, but I didn't. Mama was tugging at my heartstrings as though she was telling me good-bye.

JOURNAL ENTRY:

Dean

We circled the block several times, careful about going directly back to her place. I kept on my hat and glasses. When we were convinced that all was clear, we made a run for it. She wasted no time jumping into the shower and back out again, eager to get back to the hospital. I thought she could use a little break. "Aren't you going to eat?" I asked.

"I'll grab something on the way back up there." She shrugged her shoulders. "Or maybe in the cafeteria."

I was concerned about her state of mind and also the fact that she hadn't slept in more than twenty-four hours. "Are you sure you don't want me to go with you, or at least drive you back?"

"I'm sure." She struggled to get her jeans buttoned. "If I can be honest, this is a lot for me all by itself. As much as I want you there, having to worry about hiding you is too much right now."

"I understand." I truly did.

"Sorry," she said. "I just need to focus."

"I know," I said. "Just call me when you're leaving; I'll wait up for you."

"I'll probably stay the night," she said, "so don't wait up. But I will call, or at least I'll try." She then realized, "Oh, wait, I don't have reception there . . ."

"Come here." I took her by the hand. "I'll get out of your hair so that you can deal with this. I'll call you to let you know that I'm all right, and if I'm not all right I'm sure you'll hear about it."

"Where are you gonna go?" she asked.

"Don't know, but you don't need to be worried about that." Part of me wanted her to tell me not to go, to stay, to wait for her to get over this tragedy or stay to help her cope. The man in me wanted her to need me around, but her mother was dying and she sure as hell didn't need to be concerned with helping a fugitive escape justice. Before she could say anything, I said, "I'll be fine." There was a knock on her door. "Are you expecting someone?"

"No." She looked scared. "Shit!"

"I'll check the peephole." I took a deep breath. "It's your boyfriend," I teased in a whisper.

"Darryl?" she asked.

"Yep."

"I'm not opening it," she whispered. "I don't have time for his drama, especially not today."

As we walked away from the door, Darryl started talking

through it like he had X-ray vision, "I know you're right there," he said. "If you know what's good for you, you'll open the door. We need to talk."

"He's so full of it." Audra dismissed him.

"Audra," Darryl called out, "I know about Dean. I was just dragged down to the police station about a Greyhound bus ticket. You need to explain this shit to me."

We looked at each other. "What the fuck!" The words came out of her mouth, but the expression was all over my face. "What did he just say?" she asked on her way to the door.

"I'll listen from the bedroom," I said.

"Audra, open the door," Darryl said. "I'm trying to help you."

I made it to the bedroom and grabbed my gun.

"Hey, what's up," she said nonchalantly as she opened the door.

"What the fuck do you have yourself involved in, Audra?" he asked her right off of the top.

"What are you talking about?"

"Where is he?" Darryl asked.

"Who?" Audra tried to play dumb. "Where is who?"

"Dean Tyson," he said. "Has he hurt you or anything?"

"What are you talking about?"

"Someone bought a Greyhound bus ticket under my name," he said. "Then that someone just so happened to look like the mufucka who killed those cops. People saw him at the station and reported it to police, and because his ticket was in my name they took me down to the station to question me, put me in a lineup, and released me," he huffed. "On the way out I see the wanted posters for Dean Tyson and that just so happened to be the same mufucka who was here on Friday night—your new man or whatever."

"Oh, my God, they know about me?" Audra freaked out.

"They never said your name, but I recognized his face," Darryl said. "What do you have to do with any of this? You know him?"

"I bought the ticket in your name on my card, so they'll know about me."

"Did he have you held hostage, or were you harboring a fugitive?" Darryl asked.

"No, not really," she said. "I just did something to help him out and got caught up in the situation, but I didn't do anything to hurt anyone." She took a deep breath. "He's not what people think he is. It was all a mistake. He didn't mean to do what he did. He hasn't hurt me; everything I've done for him was voluntary." Her voice trailed off. "I wanted to help him, but I didn't know it would end up like this."

"What the hell did you think would happen when you helped a man wanted for murder?" he asked.

She didn't answer. I heard her crying, and he kept badgering her with questions. I couldn't hide any longer. I walked down the hall with my gun pointed at him.

"What the fuck." Darryl jumped nearly a foot off of the ground when he saw me. "Aw, man, I don't want anything to do with this shit."

"Have a seat," I said and stopped at the end of the hallway, about ten feet away from him. "Sit down," I repeated.

"Sit down, Darryl," Audra cried.

"Damn," he said as he sat. "So you've been holding her hostage all this time?"

"Just tell me what you know, from start to finish," I said.

Darryl's cocky attitude fell like a cheap suit in my presence. He told us the whole story in under five minutes.

I looked at Audra. "Go throw some clothes in a bag. We have to get out of here."

"Hold up." Darryl quickly put on his superhero cap. "You're not taking her with you." He volunteered, "You can take my car and you can take my money, but you aren't taking her."

"Really?" I wanted to laugh and nominate his brave performance for an award. Instead I looked at Audra once more. "Pack some clothes, shoes, and necessities. We need to go."

"Where to?" She seemed lost. "How?"

I yelled at her, "Just throw some goddamn clothes together. We have to get out of here."

She left the room in tears and I turned my attention to Darryl. "Thanks for volunteering your car. You better not report it stolen."

"Whatever you say, man." He surrendered with his hands halfway up.

I said, "This is the least you can do for her after all you've put her through."

"You don't know shit about our relationship."

"Oh, yeah?" I positioned the gun just inches away from his trembling temple. "I know that you're bonin' her best friend." He didn't say a word. "Now, we can keep that between the two of us, or I can call her in here, hand her this gun, and tell her what you've really been up to. So, thanks for the car and your fuckin' wallet," I said. "Stand up and empty your pockets."

He put the contents of his pockets onto the coffee table, including his phone and his wallet. "How much money you have on you?"

"I don't know, man," he whined.

"Toss me the wallet." I searched it and found eight hundred dollars. "Thanks." I pocketed the money.

"C'mon, that's my rent money; I'm already late. What am I supposed to do now?"

"Ask Casey. It seems she'd do anything for you."

In twenty minutes, the three of us were out of the door and in Darryl's car. As we exited the area, two black-and-whites, followed by two unmarked police cars, were turning down her street. It seemed like we got out just in time. Audra was driving and I sat in the back with Darryl to keep an eye on him.

"I know we've had our differences, but I thank you for not telling the police the things you could've." Audra's voice shook as she spoke to Darryl. "I'd appreciate it if you don't mention any of this to anyone. I promise you that as soon as this all clears up, we'll have a long talk about it." She was too nice to this jerk-off. "Darryl," she went on explaining, "it's not what you think. I promise to take care of your car. I'll mail the key back with the address where you can find it."

We pulled up in front of the mall to drop Darryl off. "Please take care of her," Darryl said to me. "I'm letting you take my car and my money. All I ask is that you take care of her." He turned to her and said, "I'm sorry for everything I put you through. Be safe, baby."

Audra relinquished the driver's seat to me and we hit Florida Turnpike. "So after we leave the hospital, where are we going?"

"We're *not* going to the hospital!" I was sorry to inform her.

"What do you mean we're not going to the hospital?" She gawked at me. "That was the whole plan. I told you that I was just going home to shower and change and then I was going back to the hospital."

"That was before we knew the police were looking for you. Our plans have to change," I said. "We can't go to the hospital now."

"We have to go the hospital," she said. "I at least need to see her before we go."

"Didn't you see those squad cars and unmarked vehicles turn down your street?" I asked. "They are looking for *you*."

"We don't know that for sure," she said.

"Audra, I'm positive they now know where you work, where you live, what you eat, what size panties you wear, so they know that your mom is in the hospital. They're waiting on you to show up, and the minute you do—they'll have you."

"I don't care!" she shouted. "That's a chance I'm willing

to take—I need to see Mama. If I have to be arrested just to do so, then I will." Audra started freaking out. "I knew I should've turned your ass in the first chance I got. Now look at me, I'm all fucked up and involved in this bullshit with you. I let you take my whole goddamn life away." She cried. "I didn't kill anybody. I don't have to run. I'll tell them that you held me hostage and used my computer and my credit card to buy that ticket on your own, or you held a gun to my head and made me buy it."

"Yeah, why don't you go ahead and do that, Ms. Clever?" I was more than pissed. "And when you're done, explain to them why you went to work on Monday instead of to the police station and came back home with me still there," I said. "Don't be stupid. They'll see right through anything you have to say." I shrugged my shoulders. "But if that is what you want, then go ahead." Awkward silence was our backseat passenger until I left the highway at the hospital's exit and pulled into a shopping plaza. "I can't risk pulling up in front of the hospital, so I have to let you out here."

"What a gentleman." She cried and shook her head. "I can't believe you."

"What do you want me to do?" I asked.

"You're just going to drop me off and let me go down by myself?" she shouted. "You don't give a damn about me or my situation. All you care about is getting away, to hell with the fact that my mother is dying!"

"I care that your mother is dying." I said. "I put my life in jeopardy today to come to the hospital."

"You did." She sniffled. "But if I leave with you I may never see her alive again."

"And if you go to the hospital and get arrested you damn sure won't see her alive again." I broke it to her hard. "We can try to get away from here and still have our freedom, or we can walk into the hospital and lose it forever." I was scared, but my mind was made up. "I don't know where we'll end up, but I promise you that when things aren't so hot on us I will bring you back to see your mother—no matter how long it takes."

"That could take years, Dean." She sobbed.

"I know," I admitted. "But I'll keep my promise."

She panicked a little. "What if she's dead by then?"

"Sorry to say this, but she'll die even if you're in prison," I said. "The choice is yours."

"All right, I know we need to run. Can't I just to say good-bye to her quickly?" she asked.

"Don't think with your heart; think with your head, Audra." I was trying not to get angry. "I'd do almost anything to go and see Destiny, but I can't."

As she sobbed, I reached over and rubbed her back. I could only imagine what she was feeling, and I felt pretty terrible because it was my fault. I kissed her forehead. "We're just going to drive for a while and see where we end up." I rubbed her shoulder. "There is no way I'm letting you go down for what I did," I said. "I can't do that."

"So where are we going?" she asked innocently. "Mexico, Canada, the Bahamas?"

Right then a lightbulb went off in my head. "Hmmm, not a bad idea." I reversed out of the parking space and hit the road again.

"What's not a bad idea?" she asked me.

"The Bahamas." I smiled and patted her thigh. "Someone owes me a big favor." Right away I thought back three years to how the favor came about.

Working as an executive chef had its perks. The easiest way to a rich person's heart is through his stomach. I had met many celebrities and wealthy people all because I satisfied their palates. "My compliments to the chef," they'd say, and then beg the staff to have me make an appearance. Some of them wouldn't be able to hide their shock when I, a tall, dark brotha, walked out instead of Gordon Ramsey. I always got a kick out of it. I'd be asked to personally cook for their parties or to come over and prepare a personal meal. The men wanted me to cook, but the women normally wanted me to eat . . . them.

I was hired to cook dinner for a man named Domenico Bianchi. I pulled up to his fabulous six-bedroom house on the Fort Lauderdale waterfront and wondered why and how some people got those kinds of blessings from God. However, when I realized that he was only about twenty-nine and couldn't really tell me what he did for a living, I knew God had nothing to do with it.

Inside, the house was a sight to behold. There were marble floors, chandeliers, vaulted ceilings, and leather furniture everywhere. Someone had already set the dining room table with a linen tablecloth and crisp napkins. There was a pathway of rose petals and candles from the door all the way to the living room, and entering the house behind me were two violinists. Domenico was preparing to ask his girlfriend to marry him.

He showed me to the kitchen and returned to the call he had on hold. "Look, babe, I'll see you tomorrow," he said. "I have something important going on tonight. I'll call you." He paused, then continued in what was supposed to be a whisper. "Of course I've thought about it. Have you been thinking about sucking my cock?" He laughed. "I hope so, because tomorrow night I'm taking your fuckin' tonsils out with it. I love you! *Ciao!*"

I prepped for about an hour and a half and was ready to cook around eight, which is when his woman arrived. She was flabbergasted. It was her birthday and she was thrilled by the evening her man had put together for her. The surprise would come later. I put the desserts in the refrigerator and packed up my things to leave. Ironically, when I opened the door there was a woman walking up to it wearing nothing but a hot pink thong.

"Wow," I said under my breath.

"Hi," she said. "Is Dom inside?"

I didn't know what to think. I doubt if he would be hiring a stripper to entertain his future wife. Who was this chick and how did she get past the gate? "Is he expecting you?" I asked.

Her perfectly round ultraperky 36 DDs answered. "Not

really, but he's always happy to see me and the girls." She looked down at her breasts.

"Huh?" I didn't hear anything she said.

"Is he here or not?" she asked.

I snapped back into reality from boobland and closed the door behind me. "No, he's not here."

"Then why would you ask if he was expecting me?" She tried looking through the glass on the French doors. "Who are you, anyway?" She looked me up and down.

"I'm a chef. He hired me to . . ." I tried to think without grabbing her mammoth mammary. "I was here to discuss a future event with him, but in the middle of our meeting he got an emergency call and had to leave. So he told me to make up the menu and leave it for him." If she didn't know that I was lying, then she was an idiot, but then who shows up to someone's house unexpectedly in a thong?"

"If I go one more week without sex I'm going to die," she said very quietly to herself.

Right then the front door opened and Dom yelled, "Hey, guy, Chef, you forgot this." With one of my aprons in his hand, Dom's eyes nearly popped out of their sockets when he saw the woman. "Holy shit."

"Dommie," the blonde cooed and ran up the stairs to him.

He put his hands up to discourage her touch. "Stacy, what are you doing here?"

"Oh, baby, I just had to see you." She walked up more stairs. "He said you were gone."

"No!" He grabbed her hand and ushered her back down

the stairs. "Never show up here uninvited and like this." He pointed at her thong. "What the fuck is this? Why would you come here like this?"

I thought quickly, trying to help him out. "I hope your mother isn't still looking outside."

"Your mother is here?" The girl tried hiding her goods with her hands.

"Yes, Ma is here. How can I have you meet her like that?" he asked. "Get out of here. You'll disgrace me."

"Dom, I'm sorry," she said. "I'll go put something on and come back so that I can meet her."

"No, forget it." He frowned. "All of your clothes look like stripper shit. I'll call you tomorrow. I'll take you someplace nice."

"Okay, baby. You promise?" she said as she raced back to her car.

"Is that what I fuckin' said?" Dom asked in frustration.

"Yes, baby, I'm sorry." Stacy got into her car and blew a couple kisses.

"Quick thinking, buddy. Thank you," Dom said once she had sped off.

"No problem, but I'm surprised I could think with those *things* in my face," I joked.

"Fuck the tits; she sucks cock like a champ," he whispered. "Dumb as fuck, though."

I laughed. "No degree needed to master that skill."

"Yes, but good looking out, man." He reached for my hand. "What's your name?"

I had told him my name twice already. "Dean. No problem. I didn't want you getting caught."

"I owe you one," he said.

"Naw man." He slapped fives with me. "Always glad to help a dude out."

"I appreciate it." he said, and then asked, "Do you like fishing?"

It wasn't my favorite pastime, but I knew it could involve one of his tight-ass boats, so I answered, "Yeah, I fish."

"Cool. Me and a few of my buddies are going to Bimini on Saturday. Wanna ride?"

Hell, yeah is what my mouth wanted to say. "Yeah, sure," I said.

"Cool," he said. "Be here at five in the morning."

"Thanks, man, I will." We talked a little more before his girl opened the door to assure herself that things were all right.

Saturday we took his black-and-red Eliminator 380 Eagle XP speedboat to Bimini in the Bahamas. The ride was awesome, and in less than an hour and a half we were there. Bimini was only about fifty miles from Miami—a fifteen-minute plane ride.

Most of the natives knew Dom. The women looked at him like they wanted a piece of him, and the men all wanted to buy him drinks.

"There he is," an excited native shouted. "Dom the Italian bomb."

"Larry," Dom shouted as he stood up, smiling from ear to ear and reaching for the man's hand.

* * *

Dom and I became the best of friends, and I didn't have to ask questions to learn that he was involved in drug trafficking and his family had ties to organized crime. After a year of us being cool, he begged me to get the owner of the restaurant I worked at to launder money for him. Carlos was more than willing. The business had taken a big financial loss. Days later I gave him two hundred thousand dollars in cash from Dom. Carlos wrote me a check for twenty grand as Dom instructed, one to Dom for a hundred and fifty thousand, and kept thirty g's for himself just for picking up the pen.

It's been three years now, and we've done this six or seven times, not always with that much money, but whatever it was, I always got a slice. However, the last time, Dom needed my share and his for an investment and told me that he'd pay me for my involvement later, that was about two months ago. I had seen him several times since the deal went down but never brought it up. So he still owed me.

I lowered the window to Darryl's car and pressed the buzzer. "Who is it?" Dom asked.

"This is Dino, the brotha muthafucka!" With a nervous smile and a sloppy Italian accent, I said the nickname his uncle Neko had given me.

"What?" He had to be sure. "Dino?"

"Yeah, man," I said.

"No fuckin' way," he said as the buzzer went off. "Bring your black ass in here."

If anyone wouldn't judge me, it was Dom. The stories he shared with me about his dad, uncles, and cousins were horrendous. What I had done wouldn't hold a candle to them. Before I could pull up to the house, Dom was outside waiting on me.

"Holy shit!" he said as though he had seen a ghost in the car window. He pulled me out and kissed both my cheeks. He hugged me like I was his blood brother. "How the fuck are you?"

"Not good, man," I said. "I really fucked up, but I guess you already know."

"I know. Let's talk." He was trying to get me into the house.

"Wait." I stopped at the bottom of the stairs. I had told Audra not to get out of the car until I told her to, until I spoke to Dom. "I have someone with me."

"Who?" He looked back at the car suspiciously.

I sighed. "A woman. Her name is Audra."

"Why the fuck are you rolling with pussy right now?" he asked. "Do you know how much trouble you're in?"

"She's been helping me, so she's involved too. She's good people, she's cool," I said. "Long story, but she has nowhere else to go but with me."

"Bring her out, then," he said. "If she's good people with you, then she's good people with me."

I went back and got Audra and introduced them. Then we all walked in and sat down, and I told Dom the entire story—Destiny, Hershel, the cops, the shooting, and Audra.

"So what do you need from me?" he asked without me having to ask him for help.

"We need to disappear," I said.

"I'm a magician, baby." He laughed. "What else?"

"The money that you were supposed to give me, just open up a trust fund for Destiny, so that when she's older . . ."

"Consider it done." He waved me off. "That's my niece as far as I'm concerned, and she'll never want for nothing," he said. "And Hershel? Done!"

"Thanks, man." I wanted to cry. "The hardest part about this was leaving her and not knowing if I'd see her again."

"I know, but stay focused; we'll deal with that later," he said. "We have to get you out of here ASAP. I can't even tell the family that you're here. Tony fucked up and there is some heat on us already. They'll kill me if they know you came here."

"Sorry. You were the only person I could turn to," I said.

"No problem, man," he said. "Wanna go hang out in Bimini at the house for a while?"

That was exactly what I was hoping he'd suggest. "That would be perfect."

"Great!" he said. "I'll have Larry bring some groceries by for you. The boat is all gassed up; we can leave in a few hours if you want, or in the morning, but I suggest we get there when it's dark."

"Whatever you wanna do is fine by me," I said. "I just need some clothes."

"Go in my closet and take your pick, but you're going to look Italian like a muthafucka." We all laughed.

*   *   *

Dom had something to do and told us to make ourselves at home for an hour and we'd leave as soon as he returned. He never did get married so he had a lot of women's clothing left over from the breakup. He told Audra she could have anything she wanted, but urged her to wash everything before wearing it. After rummaging through clothes sizes 0 to 4, she was able to find some things in what she called "real women" sizes, but even then she said that everything would be a tight fit. We put all of our things in a suitcase and waited for Dom.

I made some sandwiches, and as we ate my mind started to run wild. Dom's hour was up and I started thinking. What if Dom is turning me in for the reward? I had seen him do some pretty unscrupulous things for money. He was my friend, but what was the real story about where he had disappeared to? I was paranoid. I wanted to bring it up to Audra, but I didn't want to ring her alarm. I would give him about fifteen more minutes, and then we were taking off in Darryl's car.

During minute thirteen I was honest with her. "I think we better go."

"What?" she asked. "What do you mean?"

"I don't like all this waiting," I said. "It's making me uncomfortable."

"You're not serious, are you?" She laughed. "This is the only hope we have. You said that he's like a brother to you, right?"

"It's just that all of this waiting around stuff isn't sitting well with me."

"He's involved in a lot of dirt, so why would he go to the

police, inviting them into his life and all the shit he's done?"
She made a lot of sense. I chilled, and about ten minutes later
the French doors opened and I nearly died. It wasn't Dom
who walked in, it was my baby girl, Destiny.

She looked from side to side and then spotted me sitting
at the dining room table. "Daddy?" She couldn't believe her
eyes. "Daddy!" she yelled.

"Destiny." We trotted toward each other. In the few
seconds it took to get to her I noticed everything, her one-
tooth-missing smile, her ponytails, her honey brown skin, her
skinny long legs—everything. I squeezed her. I was crying,
my heart was racing, and I was trembling. I hadn't been happier in my life. This moment surpassed even the day she was
born. I had thought I would never see her again.

"Baby, I love you!" I said into her little ear. "I love you so
much."

"I love you too, Daddy," she said, holding me around the
neck and crying.

"Are you okay?" I asked her. "Are you all right?"

"I am now." She whimpered. "Now that I see you I'm
okay."

That was my baby. Even at such a young age, she was
always concerned about me. She was a real daddy's girl, and
it seemed only yesterday I was crossing my fingers and saying, "No doo-doo, please no doo-doo," when I changed her
diapers.

"I love you, baby girl," I said again, still holding on to her.

"I love you too."

She crawled onto my lap. I stared into her face, unable to speak. "What have you heard about me?" I asked her.

"What do you mean?" she asked innocently.

I struggled to find the right words. "Has your mom or anyone told you that I did something that might be considered bad?"

"No. People just keep asking me if I know where you are or have you called me and if I see you or talk to you that I need to let someone know." She shrugged her shoulders. "Why?"

"Does your mom tell you that too?" I had to know.

She shook her head. "She said that if I see you or talk to you that it was *my* business and not to tell anybody, not even *her* if I don't want to."

"Good," I said. "I want you to listen to Mommy on this one."

"Okay," she said.

I took a deep breath. "You're probably not going to see me again for a while."

"Why?" She hugged me.

"Because I made a big bad mistake, and if certain people know where I am they'll . . ." I didn't know what else to say.

"But you always tell me that if I make a mistake to just concentrate on doing it right and to start over," she said.

"I know, but it's not that kind of mistake, honey." I said.

"A mistake is a mistake, Daddy. You can't let people keep you away from me. That's not fair." She looked deep into my eyes and said, "I don't want to go without seeing you this long ever again."

There were no words that would make a seven-year-old understand this. "Remember how I told you that Grandpa is in your heart even though you don't get to see him and that he loves you and thinks of you every day from heaven?"

"Yes." She nodded. "I remember."

I took a deep breath. "Well, that's how it'll be with you and me for a while, only I don't know how long."

"But Grandpa is dead, Daddy." She hugged me tight. "I saw him in the casket. Daddy, I don't want you to die. Please, Daddy, don't . . ."

I made her look right into my face. "Sweetheart, I am alive and I am breathing. I am talking to you. I am alive, right?"

"Yes." She sniffled.

"Just because you won't see me a lot doesn't mean that I am not alive." I kissed her forehead. "I'll be thinking of you every day. I won't be living in Florida, but I'll be even closer—I'll be living in your heart. You won't see me, but I can't get any closer than that, right?"

"You won't be in heaven, though, right?"

"I'll be right here on earth but just not close enough to see you every day."

"I think I get it. My friend Brandon's dad lives in Washington, the one where the White House is, he goes to see him sometimes but he doesn't see him every day or anything like that and then sometimes his dad comes here and they do fun things together."

"Cool," I said. "So it'll be something like that, but I don't know exactly when I'll see you again. But no matter how long it takes, always remember that you will see me again and that I love you more than I've ever loved anyone in my life."

"I love you more than I've ever loved anyone ever before in my life too."

"Even Teddyboo?" I joked about her favorite stuffed animal.

"A million times more than Teddyboo!"

"That means the world to me, baby." I kissed her at least a hundred times before I noticed Audra sitting at the dining room table draped in tears.

"Daddy, why is she crying?" Destiny whispered.

"She's my friend and her mother is sick and in the hospital," I told her. "I bet she'd like it if you gave her a big hug and said a few nice things about her mother feeling better."

"You think so?" she asked.

"Yes," I said. "Her name is Audra."

Destiny slowly walked over to the table. "Miss Audra?" She approached carefully. "I'm sorry that your mama isn't feeling well now, but I'm sure she will in the morning or in a few days. One time my mom was in the hospital, they gave her some shots in her arms and some pills and soon we were all back home." She touched Audra's arm. "Would you like a hug?"

"Sure I would, honey." Audra embraced her. She tried to smile, but her tears were overwhelming. "Thank you so much, sweetheart."

Dom allowed us to spend about an hour together before he had to take her back to Tanisha, who was waiting at a nearby shopping mall. I found out that Hershel hadn't touched her again. Tanisha had actually put him out. The fact that he was still breathing made me want to risk it all just to get to him. Dom calmed me down. "I promise you that his mother, if the fuckin' perv has one, will be wearing a black dress by the weekend, and I will see to it that Tanisha get Des some counseling or I will myself."

I walked Destiny out to the car. I knelt down to look directly into her face. "Remember what I said to you, Destiny. I will always love you and I will think of you forever and ever. . . all the time."

"Me too, Daddy." She wrapped her arms around my neck. "I love you!"

"Always do things that will make me smile, because I will feel it in my heart," I said.

"You will?" She was amazed. "How does it feel?"

"My heart will have the same feeling your mouth does when it smiles."

"So your heart will smile?" she asked.

"Yes, baby." I held on to her. "My heart will smile."

"I'll remember that, because I would want you to feel your heart smiling," she said. "I love you."

"I love you too, Destiny." I fixed her seat belt and touched her soft little face. "It may not be tomorrow, next week, or next year, but you *will* see me again. Just be patient and know that this is not the way I want it, but this is the way that things have to be for right now."

"I know. You've always told me that you wish you could see me every day." She held my hand. "You made a mistake, it's not your fault. I understand, Daddy."

"Thank you, baby." I said. "I love you!"

"I love you too, Daddy."

I could stand there holding her little hand forever, but finger by finger we let go of each other, and before I knew it I had the strength to close the door and watch Dom drive away with my heart. I stood there in the driveway for several minutes with tears bathing my face.

JOURNAL ENTRY:

Audra

About an hour after Destiny left, we boarded Dom's boat and in pitch darkness rode to what seemed like nowhere. We were going so fast that several times I found myself holding on to various parts of the boat, trying to keep from flying out. I held on to my life vest and wondered what my life in the Bahamas would be like. I was a wanted woman leaving the United States on a speedboat.

I couldn't help thinking of my family and how they would feel when they heard what I was involved in. I would do just about anything to let them hear my side of the story. Oddly, I found comfort in knowing that my mother wasn't in a position to know about any of this.

After riding for more than an hour, I finally saw lights speckled in the distance, and Dom screamed for us to stay down. We pulled up to a private stretch of beach with a small dock. Dean tied up the boat and Dom threw our suitcase out to him. Dom helped me off of the boat and walked us up through the beach and then a winding garden pathway to a light blue house.

They walked through the house, and I heard Dom speaking in what he thought was a whisper, "There's about seventy grand in the safe in the bedroom. It's yours." He handed Dean a set of keys. "Keep the doors locked, don't go out if you don't have to right now, and if you feel the need to, go out only at night," he advised. "When I'm coming, I'll let Larry know a day or two before." He spoke louder, "Larry is your man for anything you need."

"Are you sure that Larry is going to be cool with this?" Dean asked.

"Hell, yeah! Larry has been doing work for my family for forever," Dom said. "He's been with us through a lot, and we've done a lot for him."

"Thanks so much," Dean said. He hugged Dom. "I wouldn't know what to do without you Dom."

"That's why you're *not* without me," he said.

I had a request for Dom, but I didn't know how to ask. He hardly talked to me, and even when he wanted to know something about me he'd ask Dean, as though he was my personal translator. I didn't know how to fix my mouth to ask him for a favor. His swag was very arrogant, cocky, and aggressive. "Ummm, Dom," I butted in to their thank-you fest. "May I ask you to do something for me?"

He looked at Dean like *you better keep this chick in line.* He turned to me. "What's up?"

I pulled a card from my pocket and tried not to cry. "My mom was critically injured in an automobile accident a few days ago. She's in ICU at Christ Regional." I took a deep breath. "This card has the number of an old high school friend. He doesn't live in Miami anymore. He's just visiting for a few days, so I don't think anyone will be on him." I paused . . . Screw it, I had to be real, the tears poured out. "Do you think you can call him every once in a while to find out how my mom is doing and just let me know whenever you come over here?"

"Sure." He walked over to me. "I can do that for you."

"Thanks." I didn't want a hug or a pat on the back or anything, and he didn't offer. His words were more than enough. "Thanks so much." I advised that he call and just say that he was inquiring about Mrs. Doris's health. He assured me that he knew how to handle things and probably wouldn't have to call at all.

When Dom disappeared into the night, Dean and I retired to the bedroom. It was after midnight and we were in a tropical paradise, but there was nothing sultry or sexy about it. We lay side by side staring up at the ceiling, and we both knew there would be no hot, steamy, passionate sex tonight or any night in the immediate future. Horny? What was that? I was scared and sick to my stomach. I was on the run and I was crying . . . again.

"I'm sorry I got you into this," he said.

"I got myself into this." I scolded myself. "I should've just been your prisoner, but instead I was a fool and fell for you and started helping you—"

"You fell for me?" he asked. I didn't even remember saying it, but was that the only thing he got from what I said?

"Did I say that?" I asked.

"I thought you did." He shrugged.

"Oh." I tried to continue, "So what I should've done was—"

"Did you fall for me, though?" he asked, interrupting me once more.

"I . . ." I thought for a second. "I don't know. I don't know if this is the time to even think about something like that."

"Really?" He chuckled. "So what should we be thinking about?"

"The reality of the situation we're in." I looked over at him. "We're on the run."

"I've been on the run since we've met so nothing has changed for me. So I guess that's why it's easy for me to think about wearing your thighs around my face like an oxygen mask right now."

"What?" I was a little outraged. "You are lying here thinking about sex?"

"I'm lying here thinking about sucking on that fat, juicy clit of yours."

"You can't be serious." I was upset.

"I am."

"You must be out of your fuckin' mind," I said in a huff. "Do you actually think that I can get wet right now?"

"I know you can." He moved over me. "I'm willing to show you."

"Dean, I have a lot on my mind," I said. I wasn't about to let him go down on me. How could he even be in the mood? He smiled at me, thinking that I was trying to play hard to get. He nibbled on my neck. "Stop!"

"C'mon, baby!" he said. "Shit can go extremely wrong for us at any moment, so why not just enjoy ourselves?" He caressed my breast and laughed.

"I don't find this funny."

"You might as well let me eat that pussy," he joked. "The girls in the pen won't do it like me."

"Get off me." I pushed him off and hopped out of bed. "Thanks for being such a comfort." I walked out of the room.

I sat on the sofa in the living room and cried until the sun came up. At some point my body just couldn't take it anymore, and I fell asleep. When I woke up, Dean was sitting across from me with his legs crossed up on the coffee table drinking what looked like lemonade. My eyes weren't half opened yet when he said, "I'm very sorry for my behavior last night."

I sat up and gawked at him and then looked around the place. "I guess I wasn't dreaming," I said.

"No. We're both living a nightmare in paradise."

"Yeah." I sniffed the air; something smelled great. "You cooked?"

"Yeah," he said. "I used what was in the kitchen and made some chicken souse. Would you like some?"

"Yes, thank you. It smells great." I stood. "But let me get showered and everything first."

"Cool." He beat around the bush a little. "Did you hear me say sorry?"

"Yes." I was curt.

"I am very sorry," he said and stood to look directly into my face. "I shouldn't have been so insensitive. It's just that I was trying to find a way to make you forget everything. I just wanted to make you feel better for a few minutes." He struggled with his words. "I can't take you anywhere, I can't buy you anything nice, I can't promise you a rose garden. So that was all I had, just your body and mine. I'm a man—that's what I think about."

"You could've held me, Dean."

"I know." He pleaded with his eyes. "But this is the first time in my life that I have gotten someone into something that I cannot help her get out of. I can't tell you how much I hate myself right now." He walked away from me. "If turning myself in meant you being free of all of this, I would." He turned back toward me and asked, "Do you believe that?"

"Yes." I believed it.

"I am so sorry that I involved you in this, and I am so sorry that I wasn't the man you needed last night," he said. "I am even sorry that I am not man enough to give myself up—"

"That would just be stupid, not manly."

His eyes pierced mine, drawing me in to say something powerful. "If you were serious about going to the hospital, I would've gone with you," he said. "I wouldn't have left you to go down alone. I know I said that I would've let you go, but I wouldn't have. In these last few days you have done so much for me and you have started to mean so much to me that there is no way I would've or could've let you go." Dean continued, "So it was go down with you or run away with you." He grabbed my hand, kissed it, and finished what he had to say. "I promise to take care of you, Audra, and not because I feel obligated to but because I . . ." He stopped himself. "I've developed real feelings for you. I really and truly like you a lot."

That was a mouthful. It sounded like he was in love with me. I wanted to tell him I felt the same. I opened my mouth several times but my mind just kept saying, *You've known this man for a week, you must be out of your cotton-pickin' mind.* Instead I smiled at him.

Dean looked a little disappointed that I didn't reply, but he didn't say it.

While I was in the shower, I thought back to the last man who had said something that made me feel this flustered and giddy. It was Gary! Darryl always said nice things, but because his actions showed how he really felt, I took it with a grain of salt. With Dean, however, I knew he meant everything he said.

"Did I say something wrong?" Dean startled me from outside the shower curtain.

"No." I grimaced nervously. "Why do you ask?"

"Well, you ran away like you saw a ghost," Dean said.

"Maybe I did," I said.

"How so?"

I took a deep breath. "It's been a long time since a man has said something like what I think you were trying to say."

"Trying to say?" he asked. "I said exactly what I meant. I thought I was clear."

I didn't know where this was going. Darryl had my mind all jacked up. "I'm sorry. I just didn't know how to take what you were saying. I haven't had a man talk to me like that in a good while."

"Did you think I was saying that I loved you?" he said, pulling the curtain back.

I couldn't win, so I just kept it real. "Yes, that's what I thought you were trying to say."

He stepped into the shower, grabbed me from behind, and whispered into my ear, "That's exactly what I was trying to say, but I've been through a lot and can't bring myself to, especially after only knowing you for days." He kissed my wet shoulder. "But yes, that's how I feel about you."

I slowly turned to face him, "That's how I feel about you too." I smiled. "I can't say it either."

"How about we just say 'it,' then?" He looked at me and said the single word. "It!"

"It too." I buried my head in his chest.

I guess he remembered what I'd said earlier about not being up to sex, so after our embrace he reluctantly left me in the shower. However, this time it was me who wanted him touching me or tracing my goods with his tongue. But I didn't want to weaken my words by giving in.

Sitting down to a steaming bowl of chicken souse and Bahamian bread helped me to relax. The first spoonful made me want to shout hallelujah. It was seasoned to perfection, the chicken was right on point, and he had squeezed a lime into the broth. When I was nearly done, he sat across from me and smiled.

"What's the smile for?" I inquired.

"Shit, don't you think we can both use smiles today?" He laughed, and after a slight pause said, "I was smiling because I think you're beautiful and there is no one else I would rather be in this situation with."

I blushed. "That's sweet."

"That's the truth," he said. "Don't get me wrong, though. I would rather not be in this situation period, but if I absolutely must be in it, sitting across from a face like yours makes it a little easier."

"Not being in the situation period would mean we wouldn't have met. What would you say to that?"

"Maybe you would've come into the restaurant."

I flirted. "But you would've been in the kitchen."

"I peek out from time to time," he said.

"Hmmm." I smiled. "Maybe I would've sent my compliments to the chef."

"Maybe," he answered. "And I would've come out and introduced myself." He stood up and walked around to me. "Hellow, my name is Chef Dean Tyson, and I'm happy to hear that you are enjoying your meal."

"I am, Chef." I put down my spoon and shook his hand. "It

seems like it would be a pleasure to put anything in my mouth that was touched by your hands."

"I don't and won't doubt that." He playfully cleared his throat. "Your name?"

"Audra." I said. "Chef, what—"

"Please call me Dean," he interrupted.

"Excuse me." I blushed. "Dean, what is the secret ingredient in this souse?"

"That I cannot reveal to you, Audra," he said with a sexy grin.

"Sure you can." I batted my lashes at him. "I'd really like to make this for myself from time to time."

"Would you?" he asked.

"Yes, I would love to," I said.

"Well, I'm sorry, but I can't give you my recipe," he whispered, "so how do you suggest we get around that?"

I pretended to think for a few seconds. "You could always come over and cook at my place."

"Is that right?" He smiled. "You'd allow me to come over to your place, turn on your burners, and light your fire?"

"Light my fire, huh?" I repeated slowly.

"Right up under you."

I groaned softly. "And what would I owe you for your personal catering?"

He pretended to calculate something. "All I ask in return is some super *head*, baby." We both fell out laughing.

"That's wrong." I giggled. "You'd get punched in the face in real life."

"Naw. In real life I would've gotten some super head," he teased.

"Mmm, you might have. This souse is mighty good."

"Freak!"

"Freak?" I smiled. "I'll show you a freak."

"Show me." Dean winked at me. "Show me a freak."

"Come here," I beckoned. "Take off your pants."

Nothing was going to change, so I decided to get mine.

I fell to my knees in front of him, grabbed his pants, and said, "Laundry." I got up and ran into the bedroom with him still standing there stroking himself and looking confused.

"Laundry?" He laughed and ran after me. "That was wrong."

"Sorry," I said to Dean, already up under the sheets.

I lay in his arms and listened to the waves hitting the shore. The seagulls seemed to vie for our attention and harmonized with the thunderous waters, boat engines roared in the distance, and soon we were both riding on waves of tranquility.

I wasn't thinking of anything. I was just enjoying the sounds of paradise. I inhaled the air of peacefulness. Suddenly there was an earth-shattering knock at the door. Dean and I were both tossed back into reality. I jumped up. "Who is that?"

"I don't know," he said, sitting up and putting on his pants. "You stay in here and I'll check it out."

JOURNAL ENTRY:

Dean

I looked through the peephole and then opened the door. Larry was standing there with grocery bags. "Wow," I said as I grabbed the ones on the ground.

"What's up, Dino?" He smiled.

"Nothing much, man," I said as I walked to the kitchen. "Just trying to stay down."

Larry laughed. "I hear you!"

"Thanks," I said as I looked through the bags. "I made some chicken souse. You want some?"

"Hell, yeah." He grabbed a bowl and slammed it onto the counter. "You should know you don't have to ask me nothin' like dat."

"Had to make sure." I laughed.

"Aw, man, shut your mouth," Larry said with a chuckle as I took up the souse and handed him a full bowl and two slices of bread. "I was wondering how long it was going to be before you got here."

"Yeah?" Suddenly I felt the need to explain what I had done and why I was there. "This is all a big mistake Larry, I was—"

"Stop right there," he said. "You don't have nothin' to explain to me. I've gotten to know you over these years you've been here with Dom, and as soon as I heard what went down I knew that wasn't the Dean I knew. I already know the deal; I don't need to hear the story. I got your back."

"Thanks, man," It felt good to hear that. "Thanks a lot."

Larry waved me off and asked. "You want me to have a hot plate brought over to you?"

"No, I'm good," I said "I still have half a pot of souse left."

He winked. "I'm talking about a *real* hot plate."

"Oh." I understood. He was talking about a woman or several women. "No," I whispered, "I have someone here with me."

"Oh." Larry covered up his mouth like a scolded child and looked around. "Sorry."

"No problem," I assured him. "Let me introduce you."

"I don't have to meet her right now if she's lying down or something," he said.

"Naw, she's up." I said. "Audra, come here. There's someone I want you to meet."

The door opened and in walked my future. "Baby, this is . . ."

"Larry." He offered his hand to her.

"Audra," she said. "Nice to meet you."

"You too," Larry said. "All right," he continued, looking at me, "in the situation that y'all in y'all can't talk to everybody. Right now I know her name and that she is from Miami, so if I happened to see something on TV, you just confirmed it to me and I'm running to the phone to get the reward."

"True," I said. "You're right."

"I know," Larry said in a cocky tone. "You two need new names that ya need to start callin' each other, because everybody knows that Dean and Audra are on the run together."

"How did you know that?" Audra asked.

"It was on the news this morning," he said. "You didn't know?"

"No." She sat down at the table next to Larry. "I mean, I knew that they knew something by now, but I didn't expect to be on the news." A worried look replaced her cute smile.

"The way I see it, everybody gets their fifteen minutes of fame. It can be good or it can be bad, but the one thing about it is that it's fifteen minutes and it'll be up in no time, or as soon as somebody else replaces you." He tried to be encouraging. "Stay out of the limelight and soon you'll be just a memory."

It seemed like Larry either had experience with what we were going through or he had helped others in the past, because he sure was knowledgeable. When he left, Audra turned on the television to nervously await the 5 o'clock news report in Miami. Bimini was so close to Florida that picking up all of the local South Florida channels wasn't a problem. The minute the news came on she screamed for me.

I came out of the bathroom and thanked God that I was no longer the headliner. Surprisingly, we weren't even mentioned before the first two commercial breaks, but after those messages, we were up.

The reporter rambled on, "There is an interesting new lead in the Turnpike Cop Killer saga." She paused as Audra's picture popped up on screen, and Audra sighed. "Police are looking for this woman, Audra Chandler, in connection with Dean Tyson, the man suspected of killing two state troopers. A credit card owned by Chandler was used to purchase a bus ticket to Seattle, Washington, for the suspect. It is also believed that the suspect lived with Chandler for several days after the killings. Police initially thought that Chandler was taken hostage by Tyson, but when it was learned that Chandler showed up for work on Monday, business as usual, police began considering her a person of interest in regard to this crime. Now it is believed that the two are on the run together. If you know Chandler or Tyson's whereabouts, police are encouraging you to contact Miami-Dade Crime Stoppers at the number at the bottom of the screen. A fifty-thousand-dollar reward will be given for any information leading to an arrest."

"If your family and friends really know you, then they'll know that you were trying to do something good." I tried to be of some comfort. "Maybe somehow we can get a message to them." Of course that wouldn't be smart.

"I'm just glad Mama doesn't know about any of this," she said.

"Maybe she does. Maybe she's up walking and throwing a fit about this."

She smiled. "Yeah, wouldn't that be something?"

"Can't believe that I got you to smile so soon after that news report," I teased.

"I can't believe it either," she said. "And I can't believe that they used that picture on the news. I had about a half inch of new growth and needed a perm."

Several long, nervous weeks went by, but together we made the best of them. Though we were trying to escape time in prison, we were in a cell of our own, the house. We were inside on lockdown every day. We ventured outside for about thirty minutes daily, even less than the "yard" time given to inmates. We didn't eat like prisoners, though. Larry brought us freshly caught seafood almost every day and I was cooking up a storm. We hadn't heard from Dom since he left, and we were both trying to keep in mind that no news was good news.

"Audra, I'm going out to the beach," I yelled back to the laundry room where she was putting a new load in. "You hear me?"

"Yeah!" she shouted back.

It was close to sunset. I donned a straw hat and sandals and walked out through the garden until I was on the sandy beach. I sat down, stuck my finger in the sand, and drew what was supposed to be a bird, but it looked more like Mr. Potato Head with a sharp nose.

The sunset was awesome, and I had come to truly

appreciate the incredible arrangement of colors associated with it. I had never paid it much attention before. I now had the opportunity to watch the golden sun fade into the deep blue sea every day on a private beach on a tropical island. Under different circumstances I would have said, "This is the life!"

Audra, though worried and frequently tearful, had learned to laugh again. She was a little more at peace with our situation, but she still watched the news daily to see what was up. Thankfully, for a week and a half there had been no mention of the black Bonnie and Clyde. Fortunately for us, criminals were running untamed in the streets of Miami.

I lay back on my hands, closed my eyes, and enjoyed the ocean breeze. I thought about Destiny and felt my heart smile as I promised her it would. I was hoping that she was somewhere safe and smiling back at me. The thought of letting go of her tiny hand crept up into my mind and tried to steal my joy, but I didn't let it. Instead I focused on how good it felt to hold her little hand. My smile dipped into a dark ocean, just like the sun had, when what Hershel did came to mind. How could a man be so sick? I just hoped and prayed that my baby would recover from what had happened and lead a normal life. And as hateful and vengeful as this may sound, I hoped that Dom would keep his promise to stick a fork in Hershel. I no longer had a life, and neither should he.

I tried to shake the thoughts by listening to the ocean waves once again. I breathed in through my nose and out through my mouth several times. I felt great. And things only got better when I felt her lips . . . She pressed them against mine and then sucked them into her mouth. She smelled great, like mangoes or something tropical that I wanted to taste . . . badly. I fished for her tongue and pulled it into my mouth and was aroused when she moaned lightly.

"I knew you were gonna come here," she pulled away and said. "Something told me that you were coming."

I opened my eyes and nearly buried myself in the sand when I realized that I was kissing Chante. "Oh, shit!"

"Hi, baby." She giggled. "How are you?"

"I could be better." I wasn't lying.

She replied, "Well, you should be now."

Larry had told me that she had recently moved to another island. "I heard you moved," I said.

"Well, I'm thinking of moving, but I'm still here for now," she said. "I was out of town, at a nursing conference." She smiled. "I just got back today."

I looked at her, not sure of what I should do or say.

"I know the situation. Don't worry, I won't tell a single soul." She held her hand over her heart. "I promise you."

"Thanks," I said, but it didn't sit right with me. "Thanks a lot."

"As soon as I heard the news, I knew you were going to come here . . . or at least I hoped you would." She giggled. "So I couldn't help but take a peek, and here you are on the beach."

"Yep, here I am." I was at a loss for words.

"Baby, I know you didn't do what they said you did. I

know you, and that's not you." She touched my face. "And I was praying that you would come here, so as soon as I got off of the plane today I came straight here."

"I'm in a lot of trouble!" I said. "This is no time to come looking for me. You should want to be as far away from me as possible."

"No." She shook her head. "I want to be *with* you."

I had met Chante the first time I came down here with Dom. She was going to nursing school, but to pay her expenses she was also a "working girl." Dom often hired her to "entertain" us.

Over the past three years I had seen her about a dozen times when she visited Miami. She was beautiful and intelligent, and the sex was mind-blowing. I liked her very much and enjoyed our time together.

The problem was that she liked me *too* much. The last time we had been together, she started talking about "us" and our "relationship" and where it was going. I was happy with things the way they were; I didn't want it to go anywhere. She threw a fit and accused me of thinking of her only as a whore. That certainly wasn't true, but I didn't think of her as my girlfriend either.

I certainly never expected to see her again, yet here she was, snuggling up to me as if nothing had happened.

* * *

"I'll help take care of you, baby," Chante said. "You can even stay with me."

"Naw, I can't stay with you," I said but was thinking, *holy shit!* What if she switched to superbitch mode again and called the police because I was with another woman? This wasn't good. "Has anyone tried contacting you, the police or anyone?"

"I don't think so," she said. "I was in D.C. when everything happened."

"You really shouldn't be here." I looked around the secluded beach. I was trying to act overly paranoid so that she'd go away. "Someone may have followed you or something."

"I don't think so," she said. "Everyone on the plane was a native."

"I can't take any chances, Chante," I said. "This is my life we're talking about. I can't have you coming up here, plus it'll look like you're helping me, and if I get caught you could go to jail too." I tried to scare her.

"That's true," she said with a smile. "Sorry about the way things went down the last time we were together."

"Oh, you mean when you slapped the spit out of my mouth?" I asked.

She looked embarrassed. "I'm not like that. You had me so angry." She paused and took a deep breath. "I'm glad that you're okay. Maybe at night we can meet here or I can pick you up and we can go back to my place. No one will ever see you."

"We'll see." I was still trying to get rid of her. "I can't

make you any promises. I don't even know how long I'm sticking around here. I might be gone in a few days." I was frustrated. "I don't think it would be smart for you to come back around here, though. People will start to wonder what you're doing." Then I played the trump card. "If Dom finds out, he'll go ballistic." She thought Dom was the meanest guy and the biggest asshole on the planet. "He doesn't want *anyone* here."

"Fine! I'm not used to seeing or hearing from you every day, anyway, so I'll just pretend you're not here." She kissed me on the forehead. "When you want me, just get to me somehow." She stood up. "I'll do whatever you need me to do."

I looked up at the house, Audra wasn't outside. I wondered whether I should tell Audra about Chante. I didn't want to give her something new to worry about.

I walked up to the house and looked through the window. Audra was sitting on the sofa writing in the journal she encouraged us to start "sharing" together. She said that if we were ever caught, maybe it would become a book and be known as the *new and improved* greatest love story ever told. She was so corny at times, but she was my baby!

I opened the door and she looked over with a smile. "Hi, baby!" She was the type of woman I'd always wanted to come home to.

"Hi," I greeted her. "Are you writing now about how I held a gun to your head and forced you to go down on me?" I asked jokingly.

"I was actually writing a poem."

"Were you, now?" I walked over and kissed her on the arm.

"Sure. It's called 'Call Me Crazy.'" She picked the journal up and cleared her throat. "Okay, remember that this is just a poem. I'm being creative. Don't think that I'm all in love with you and stuff. All right?"

"Just read it," I said.

"Call me crazy, but I feel the future in your touch . . .
like the day we'll get married and such . . .
like when I tell you that you'll be a dad again . . .
like us being old and you still being my best friend.
You came into my life by complete surprise
You, your perfect smile and bedroom eyes.
You, the real-life Mr. Tall, Dark, and Handsome,
have stolen my heart and refuse to take the ransom.
I am a willing hostage, keep doing what you do to me.
I'll meet demands, just promise that this is where you'll always be.
Can't imagine my existence without the joy you bring.
Don't want my heart if you stop making it sing.
Call me crazy, but I keep checking my finger for a ring . . .
'cause I swear I love you like Clair loved Bill.
White house and picket fence, flowers on the windowsill . . .
But what if we can't be the Huxtables?
Will you be down with the comfortables?
Because if you're my Martin I could be Gina or Coretta Scott!
Strong and silent! Yet opinionated, sexy, Super Fly, and hot.
We may not have Florence like George and Weezy,
But we got each other's back and that's 'Fo sheezy!'"

Call me crazy, but at nine o'clock hold me like we won't live to see
ten.
And when it's ten hold me like there is one minute 'til the end.
It's like we have the same heart beating in both our chests
'cause this feeling, this love, this thing riding me . . . never rests.
When you walk into a room I still have to catch my breath,
You're not my husband (yet), but I know this is 'til death.
Soul mates . . . lovers even before this life had begun . . .
All we had to do was meet, the victory was already won.
Call me crazy."

I was floored, rendered temporarily speechless, and of course, she took my silence the wrong way. "You didn't like it?"

I finally cracked the smile she was longing for and was able to talk. "Wow!"

"Wow?" she repeated. She looked at me as though her thoughts were, *This Negro better come up with another word other than wow . . . and soon.* "You gonna call me crazy?" she asked.

"I can't do that!" I answered her. "If I did, you'd have to call me the same thing and I might get offended." As I walked closer to her I tried to remember, "What was that line about Bill and Clair?"

She looked down at the book, "'Cause I swear I love you like Clair loved Bill."

"I love you too," I said as I pulled her to her feet.

She was stunned. "I love you, Dean."

"I love *you*, Audra." I lowered my lips to hers and somehow our kiss was different. It was like saying those three little words added extra sugar to our taste. It was sweet. Our lips were locked for at least ten minutes before we came up for air. "Now that I think about it, maybe you don't love me."

"Why?" Audra asked.

"Because Clair loved Heathcliff, not Bill," I schooled her.

"You are so right." She laughed. "But it sounded good at the time and then it rhymed with the other line, so it's a keeper."

"Am I a keeper?" I inquired as I pulled her into me yet again.

"You are definitely a keeper." She pecked me on the lips. "Am I a keeper, or are you just stuck with me?"

"I'm stuck *on* you!" I answered smartly.

For the rest of the evening I toyed with the idea of telling her all about Chante and even the kiss on the beach. I was afraid of making her worry about a malicious woman turning us in. She might be intimidated by the fact that I was sleeping with Chante off and on for nearly three years up until three months ago. I decided to keep the drama to a minimum and just keep my mouth closed for as long as I possibly could.

JOURNAL ENTRY:

Audra

Another week went by and I was starting to relax. I prayed for my mother every morning and every night. I couldn't make up my mind whether to think about her in the hospital or in heaven. Since I hadn't heard any word about her, I satisfied myself with fantasies of her waking up and the nurses running into her room in amazement. I imagined her stumbling out of bed or walking with a walker. I wanted to think of her in any way other than how I left her.

I woke up to the sound of clinking dishes and the scent of freshly brewed coffee. I smiled. Dean had truly been taking care of me, making me feel so comfortable. Yesterday he made me breakfast in bed, and as I inhaled that luscious caffeine aroma, I relaxed and snuggled myself awaiting his return with something delicious. However, when the bed suddenly moved, I realized that he was still in the bed.

"Dean!" I shook him to wake him up. "Honey!" I tried to keep my voice down. "Dean," I said into his ear.

"Yeah?" His eyes were still closed and he wasn't even concerned about why I was waking him up.

"Somebody is out there," I said, trembling. "Listen!"

"Okay," he said without moving a muscle, and he began to snore lightly.

"Dean." I jabbed him in his side. "Wake up."

"What?" Agitated, his eyes finally opened and he looked over at me, annoyed.

"There is somebody out there," I said nervously.

He rubbed his head. "You don't remember me waking you up last night and telling you that Dom came in?"

"No." I thought back. "When?"

He rolled over. "A little after two or something," he said and closed his eyes.

"Did he say anything about my mom?" I had to know.

"No."

"Did you ask?"

He hesitated. "No."

I couldn't believe that he didn't ask Dom about my mother. I didn't know if she was still in the hospital, if she was even still alive. "Thanks a lot." I was already out of bed and putting on my pajama bottoms. "That's all I've been talking about and you couldn't even ask him about her?" I was livid. He was thoughtless and inconsiderate. "You should know that's the first thing I would want to know."

He jumped out of the bed and toward me. "I didn't ask

because I wanted to be right next to you when you found out whatever news Dom has." He grabbed my hand. "I wanted to find out right along with you." He pulled me to him. "Chill out for a second, baby. Take a deep breath."

"I'm sorry." I took a deep breath.

I thought for a second. Dom wasn't the most caring or tactful person on the planet. Regardless of who he was talking to, Dom never bothered to filter or clean up anything he had to say. Stuff came out of his mouth like vomit. I didn't want to deal with that right now anyway.

I made myself stay in the shower longer than forty-five seconds because I was ready to know something, anything. I forced my hands to lather the washcloth with the soap, made myself wash off, and all but nailed my feet to the ground to rinse off. All in all, I think I stretched the whole shower ordeal out to about four and a half minutes. As I dressed I heard the bedroom door open and then close.

"Okay," I exclaimed. "Give it to me." Dean asked me to take a seat.

"Dom called your friend a week ago and nothing had changed with your mother." I could tell he felt uncertain about how I would react.

I was a little deflated, but at least the news wasn't worse. "At least she's still hanging in there."

"Yes. But he called back a few days ago and learned that the swelling in her brain miraculously went down. She is talking, moving, and in a regular room now."

"What?"

"She starts physical therapy in a few days and the doctors expect that within a few months, minus the bruises, she'll be one-hundred percent."

For the first time in a long time I was crying tears of joy. "Are you sure?"

"Yes!" He tried pulling me near, but I dropped to my knees and thanked God for my mother. It took me awhile to get it together, and when I did I decided to go down to the beach.

"Dino, the beach? Are you serious?" Dom looked at Dean. "What the fuck are you two thinking? You can't go out there!"

"We hardly ever do, but we get cabin fever, man," Dean tried to explain.

"Fuck cabin fever. Prison fever is a lot worse, my friend." He gawked at me. "I don't think that's smart, not at ten o'clock in the morning."

"I'm only going to sit in the sand," I protested like a disobedient child and quickly donned a straw hat and shades. "I won't be long."

"Okay." He looked at Dean as if to say, *Please control your bitch,* but I wasn't having it.

The island sun wrapped its long arms around me, embracing me like an old friend. The heavy ocean breeze was laden with salt, fried fish, and the nearby hibiscus and yellow elder, the official flower of the Bahamas. The fresh air was the perfect gift to me for the good news I had just received. I kept walking until my toes left the stone walkway and dug into the sand. I sat down and smiled out at the sea. I knew that somewhere across it my mommy longed for me, which made me feel fantastic. Even if it meant her knowing or finding out soon that I had made a dumb mistake I was happy that she was alive.

As I soaked up the sun, I saw a figure appear on the beach about fifty yards away. As it moved closer, I could tell it was a woman. I thought she would stop farther down the stretch, but she kept coming. "Oh, shit," I said to myself when she was about ten yards away, not knowing if I should get up and go. From a distance I assumed that she was a tourist, but when she got closer and I got to see her perfect creamy brown skin and beautiful exotic features, I knew she was probably a native.

"Good morning," she said cheerfully.

"Hi." I was nervous. "Good morning."

I anticipated her just passing by, but she stopped. "How you doin'?" she asked in an accent that confirmed my Bahamian suspicion.

"I'm fine." I barely looked at her.

"Are you enjoying your stay here?" she inquired, then sat on the sand facing me a few feet away.

"It's breathtaking."

"Imagine growing up and living here." She smiled.

"Must be awesome." I thought about just jumping up and leaving.

"Where are you from?" she asked.

"California," I lied. Hell, I had never even been to Cali. I figured people in the island probably didn't make it out there much, so I could tell her anything and she'd never know.

"Oh, I love California. I was out there for a conference a few weeks ago. Where are you from, L.A.?"

"No." I tried to think of the other major cities. "San Diego."

"Oh, wow, that's where my conference was." She was excited. "Have you ever been to—"

"Before you ask, I'll tell you that I actually just moved there, so I don't know all that much just yet."

"Oh, okay," she said. "It's this Italian restaurant downtown that is just superb." She changed her tone. "So, where did you live before then?"

"Iowa," I lied again. Nobody I knew ever knew anything about Iowa—only the people in Iowa know about Iowa. I could make up a city, governor, mayor, streets, and all and it'd be taken as gospel.

"I've never been there," she said.

"Don't worry, you're not missing anything." I chuckled.

She reached over and offered me her hand. "I'm Chante."

"Nice to meet you." My heart was beating triple time as I searched my database for a name to give her. "I'm Angela."

"Nice to meet you, Angela," she said. "I don't mean to ruin your private moment, but I was headed down the beach to my boss's house and needed to take a breather." Her mannerisms were strange. "I shouldn't even be walking this way. This is all privately owned by the people who own these houses. I climbed over a fence to take the shortcut." She giggled and looked up at the houses. "Are you staying in one of these homes while you're here?"

"Yes," I answered, and right as the word came out of my mouth I knew it was a mistake.

"Oh." She seemed intrigued. "Are you here alone or with family?"

"With my husband." Again, it was something else I probably shouldn't have said.

"Is that right?" she asked. "Honeymoon?"

"Yeah." I tried to fake a blush but noticed her gawking at my left hand.

"Where are the diamonds?" She smiled.

I had to think fast, but I should've been thinking smart instead. "Oh, we heard that we shouldn't wear a lot of jewelry around here." I yanked that statement from somewhere in the pits of hell.

Her eyes grew wide, and I could tell that I had offended her. "Someone said that you shouldn't flaunt your jewelry in front of us poor natives, huh?" she said angrily. "There is *nothing* you American women have that I cannot get on my own." She stood up and looked down at me. "Anything you have, I can have within a day, two at the most. Trust me."

"Oh, I didn't mean it like that," I tried to explain. "I wasn't trying to offend you . . ." She was already walking away and I was talking to her backside. Fuck her and the horse she rode in on. And then it hit me—she was walking back down the beach in the direction she sauntered in from. She said she was on her way to someplace. Something wasn't right. I headed back to the house.

I walked in on Dean, Dom, and Larry drinking beer and laughing about something. The minute I stepped through the door I felt Dom undressing me with his eyes. It wasn't a good or sexy feeling, though. It felt like if he got me alone he would do whatever he wanted, with no second thoughts. I was very uneasy in his presence. As I approached, he stared at my breasts as if he wanted to reach out and grab them. "How was the beach?" he asked.

"Nice!" I lied. "I needed the fresh air."

"Was anyone else out there?"

"No." There was no way I was telling Dom about the woman on the beach, especially since I had pissed her off. "Just me and the seagulls."

"Mmmm." He sipped from his bottle and continued to eye-fuck me. "You look very nice in that top." It was a pale yellow halter that I had gotten from the "stash" at his house the night we left. "I bought that one for this broad while we were in Cancún." He took a tour of my entire body while my man was wrapped up in conversation with Larry. "You fill it out perfectly."

"Thank you," I said, and then quickly worked on getting Dean's attention. "Honey, would you like another beer?"

"Sure!"

"Larry? Dom?" They both wanted one too. I disappeared into the kitchen to catch my breath from Dom's visual rape and also from the strange woman on the beach. I didn't know what to make of any of it. The weirdest things always happened to me. My only concern was that I couldn't afford to be making any enemies here. I couldn't even make any friends here. I regretted not jumping up and leaving the minute I saw her in the distance. I couldn't tell Dean and I definitely wasn't telling Dom, because as far as he was concerned I shouldn't have been out of the house in the first place.

I grabbed three beers and took them over to where they were sitting. "I'm gonna do some reading, guys. Have fun."

"Thanks," Dean said.

Larry had given us a box of books just in case we got bored watching television. I fell asleep, reading. I woke up after three, had lunch with the guys, and then we sat around playing dominoes for a while. I decided to throw back a few beers too. I had a nice time and lots of laughs. It was after one in the morning when Larry finally left. I started washing all of the dishes that had accumulated throughout the day, and Dean went to take a shower. Dom helped to bring the dirty things over to the sink for me. I was appreciating his help and then, wham, he came up behind me at the sink.

"You wearing this shirt brings back memories," he said as his erect penis rubbed up against my ass. "I fucked that chick from the back in it, just like this." He grabbed a handful of my ass, and I quickly turned and pushed him off of me.

"Dom, please don't touch me like that."

"Why not?" He slurred his words.

"First of all, because I don't like it, and also because Dean is your friend," I reminded him.

"I know." He laughed. "He's like my brother."

"Right. You wouldn't go touching on your brother's woman, would you?" I tried to break through into his drunken mind.

"Do you know how many of the same women we've had sex with?" he asked me. "We've shared a lot of pussy."

I was shocked. "You and Dean?"

"First time I brought him here we fucked four chicks together right there." He pointed at the living room. "We do that shit occasionally, unless it's someone of importance."

"Well, I am someone of importance." I deemed myself worthy of his respect.

"Oh, yeah?" He smiled "Who told you that?"

"I'm telling you that." I was angry. "I don't know what you all did together before, but I'm not one of those women."

"Let me get this straight. You're living in my house rent free, running from every goddamn law enforcement agent in the state of Florida, and you're telling me that I can't have that pussy?"

"Yes!" I said bluntly.

"That's where you're wrong, honey." He walked toward me, backing me into the countertop. "You owe me. I own you right now. When I tell you that I want to fuck, you need to hand that pussy over because it belongs to me."

"I love Dean," I said, "and he loves me. You should respect that."

"And all of that is wonderful." He eased up a little. "You should also be grateful to me. I'm the one checking up on your mother, feeding you, clothing you"—he laughed—"and putting a roof over your head. Shit, you're living better than you were before." His dark Italian eyes shot me a look that nearly stopped my breath. "I'm not going to campaign for your pussy.

I'm either getting it or you pack your shit. It's that simple."
His hand rubbed my pussy lips through my pants. "The next
time I come, there will be no questions asked." He turned to
walk away and then remembered. "Oh, and if you mention
this to Dino you'll . . ." He shrugged his shoulders. "You just
better not mention it."

I was shocked. *He's drunk*, I said to myself. *That didn't just
happen.*

I went straight into the shower. There was no way I wasn't
telling Dean. As soon as I walked out of the shower I pounced
on the bed where he was. "Have you and Dom had sex with
some of the same women?"

He looked utterly shocked.

"Have you and Dom boned the same chicks before?" I
broke it down for him.

"Why would you ask me that?" He seemed uncomfortable.

"Because *he* said that you did," I told him in a whisper.
"And he thinks that him helping us is an open invitation to
have sex with *me*."

"What?" He sat up quickly. "What the hell are you talking about?"

"When you were in the shower, he approached me," I said.

Dean was looking at me in disbelief. "Approached you
how?"

I didn't want to tell him that his boy outright physically
disrespected me, because I didn't want him to overreact. We
needed to stay in the house. "He came on to me."

"How?" Dean stood up. "What the fuck did he do?"

"Shh! He just said that he liked the way I looked in the top and then mentioned that you and he normally shared women and he wondered if I was down with that. But he's drunk, so please don't say anything. After I told him that I wasn't down with that, he begged me not to mention it to you. But I just wanted you to know the deal."

"I'm sorry about that, baby." He put his arms around me. "That's something we did here a few times and maybe once or twice in Miami, but never with a girlfriend or a woman I was seeing," he explained. "I would never do anything like that with you."

"So you don't think that I owe him sex because he's helping us?" I asked.

"Did he say that?" Dean got hyped.

"No." I continued to water down the story. "But that's the vibe I got from him, like I owe him something."

"You don't owe him or anyone else shit," Dean said. "I'm the one indebted to everyone. I brought you into this mess." He touched my face. "If anything, I owe you!" He kissed me. "I apologize for his drunk ass. I'll talk to him in the morning."

"No," I said. "Like I said, he's drunk . . . he was slurring and all. I'm sure he didn't mean anything and he did beg me not to tell you. He knows it was wrong."

Dean thought about it. "I won't say anything this time, but if he says something else, you better let me know."

"I will," I promised, but knew that I couldn't keep it.

Suddenly his hand crept into my underwear. "This is all *mine!*" he said as he massaged my lips a little.

"Yes, it is." I was already dripping onto him.

"Mmmm." He kissed my midthigh and pushed me back onto the bed. "Let me see if I can find something to eat in here that was better than everything else I had today."

"Think you can?" I joked. "Everything we had today was pretty delightful."

He pulled my panties to the side and quickly taunted my overripe cherry with his tongue. Everything on my mind had somehow gone away. Nothing mattered to me . . . only his touch, his tongue. "This is more than delightful," he said.

"Mmmm," I moaned. "It feels delightful too." It did. If all the men in the world would just man up and eat pussy properly, the world would be a better place. So Dean could single-handedly change the world; he was changing mine. With just the right mixture of licking, sucking, and fingering, I was watering the bed profusely.

"I love it when you get this wet," he said in between licks.

"Well, just keep doing what you do, honey," I teased.

"Your pussy is like a damn faucet," he said.

I groaned loudly, barely able to contain myself. "Come on, baby, give it to me." I was trying to pull him up onto me. I needed the rest of him. "Come on."

"You want this dick, huh?" he asked.

"You know I do," I said, breathing heavily. "And you want to give it to me."

"You think so?" He climbed up my body and I felt his rocket ready to take off.

"Yeah, you want to give it to me." I smiled. "And I'm ready to take it."

He kissed me on the neck and then my breasts, all the while

his dick teasing my gate by tap tap tapping on it. Finally, even *he* couldn't take the torture and pushed into me. We exhaled together, because we hadn't done it in over a week. I hadn't been in the mood for sex, and then my period snuck up on us. So this was the first time after a little hiatus, and feeling him within me, I didn't know how I could ever wait that long again.

"Ooooh, baby!" I whispered.

His dick slammed into my G-spot over and over again. My hands grabbed on to the sheets. I worked my waist and pushed down to meet his jabs. "Yeah, Audra, work it," he encouraged me. "Work it, baby."

I was trying to work it. I was putting it on him, but man, oh man . . . he pulled out all the way to the head and came back in with a vengeance. That made me call out so loud that I was sure the people of Bimini would gather for a town hall meeting to discuss it. "What was that ghastly scream?" they'd ask, and someone would answer, "I think there is foul play going on. Let's search the woods for the culprit."

"Whose pussy is this?" Dean asked, looking into my face intently for an answer.

"It's yours, baby." I could hardly catch my breath. Every poke went farther into me than the one before. "This is your pussy, Dean."

"Say it to me!" he demanded and started to move a little fast, truly tearing my shit to pieces. "Tell me."

"This is your pussy, Dean." I could feel myself lathering him up more and more. "Fuck this pussy, it's yours."

We went on for another couple minutes before I decided to switch to doggy style. I couldn't hold back now. He had pushed my volume button to the maximum. He held me at the waist with one hand and spanked me with the other as he fucked me like tomorrow would never come. I backed it up for as long as I could, but soon my body trembled beneath him and my eyes fought not to roll back into my head. I was coming. My knees buckled and I fell flat on my face onto the bed. Dean didn't let up. He didn't take my extra juices for granted. He rubbed his dick around in it and spanked my clit. Finally he dipped back in and kept grinding into me. My pussy was too much for even the Mighty Dean Tyson to last long, he succumbed to it . . . injecting me deep within.

Panting and nearly paralyzed, I was facing the door. I wanted some water terribly but didn't have the energy to get it. However, underneath the door I could see that I had left a light on in the hall. I'd have to get up and turn it off. I was flabbergasted when I noticed that the light became brighter, as if someone had been standing at the door a second ago shielding the light. It was probably Dom. He had been there listening the entire time. I was officially freaked out.

JOURNAL ENTRY:

Dean

I woke up the next morning feeling more refreshed than any day I could recently recall. Amazing what a woman with good pussy can do to a man's life. As I took my shower, I thought about what she had told me about Dom. I wanted to talk to him about it, but I had promised her that I would let it go. I hadn't yet had the chance to sit down and tell Dom what she meant to me. He probably thought that she was just a hookup I had gotten involved in my bullshit.

Underneath the stream of warm water I thought carefully about the situation. I couldn't afford to bring ruckus into my relationship with Dom. I needed him desperately right now, more than I'd ever needed anyone. Because of him we had money and a hiding place; if we lost those two things we'd lose our freedom and maybe our lives. At the same time, though, the thought of him hitting on Audra was sickening. Hopefully he was just being a horny drunk! At least he didn't put his hands on her. If he had, then I would lose my natural mind on his ass.

"What's up, man?" I said as I walked into the living room after getting dressed.

"Nothing!" Dom answered, flipping through the channels with his legs up on the coffee table. "I'm out of here in a few." Then he added, "I'm going to need your help with some shit I have going on in Colombia the next time I'm down here. Gonna need to take you with me."

For the most part I never got involved in the drug shit Dom had going on, and he had never asked me. I had assumed he never asked out of respect for me.

"What do you need me to do?" I asked.

"Details are still in the air. I'll let you know," he said. "I have to get out of here in a minute."

"Oh, yeah?" I was somewhat relieved that he was going so I could have more time to think about how to approach the situation or decide if there was a situation at all. "When are you coming back?"

"Don't know," Dom answered, but he wasn't really looking at me, just in my general area. "Might be back next week or something."

"Okay." I threw in a curveball. "Bring some Krispy Kreme glazed doughnuts. Audra loves those damn things."

He laughed. "Oh, yeah?"

"Yeah." I lied. "She ate a whole box the weekend I first met her."

"I like 'em too. They're especially good when you get them while that lil' light is on. Man, oh man."

"Yeah." I tried to fit in what I was trying to say without making it obvious. "Man, life is a vicious beast." I shook my head sadly, hoping he'd take the bait.

"Life is a motherfucker."

"Who would've thought I would meet the woman I could probably spend the rest of my life with *this* way?" I asked.

"Really?" He seemed shocked. "You see her *that* way?"

"Yeah." I smiled. "She's something special."

"I guess that is kind of fucked up," he said.

"Why?" I asked, hoping he was about to keep it real with me.

"It's fucked up that you would meet her this way," he said and then stood up. "It's fucked up for both of us that you would meet her *now*, because you have to stay focused, Dino. Don't let this love shit fuck with your freedom—our freedom," he snarled at me. "The minute you get too comfortable and take this for a fuckin' honeymoon is the minute the feds will be busting down the door. And guess what? This is *my* house, so guess who goes down next?" He didn't need me to answer. "Put your heart on the back burner for a minute and use your head. All that fuckin' lovey-dovey shit will make you lose track of the magnitude of this situation. Keep your eyes open." He sighed. "If you go down, I go down . . . and if I go down it's not a good day for the entire Bianchi family." He finished up. "My family has no clue that I'm helping you, so you can't let me down."

I didn't know what to say. I just stood up and hugged him for a quick second. "I won't let you down, Dom."

"Good!" he said. "Good!"

"Good morning!" Audra stepped into the room looking like something I wanted to taste again.

I said, "Mornin', babe!"

"Salutations," Dom joked.

"Anybody for coffee?" she asked on her way to the kitchen.

"Yeah, make two more cups," I answered, speaking for both of us.

"Coming right up." She giggled.

Dom held out his hand for us to slap palms. "I can see why you would want to honeymoon with her." He smiled and confessed, "She's hot."

"She's more than just hot. She is the total package."

"I hope that you're not offended by this, but yesterday I said something to her that might've crossed the line. I was drunk."

I knew that my boy had a heart. "What did you say?" I breathed a sigh of relief.

"I told her that the shirt she had on I had bought for a girl I took to Cancún. I told her that I fucked the chick wearing the shirt and she was bringing back memories because it looked good on her."

"You're a crazy bastard," I said to him jokingly. "Yeah, that was fucked-up to say, but I'll let you slide just as long as you didn't touch her."

"Of course not." He gave me the Italian do-you-think-I'm-crazy stare. "I'm sorry, man. I was drunk and horny. Forgive me."

"Forgiven," I said. "Forgiven."

When Audra came back with three coffees on a tray, he

let her know that he told me what he had said to her the day before and that he was sorry. She accepted his apology, but I could tell she didn't think he was sincere. She just grinned and coped with him to keep the peace. Within the hour Dom was gone. We stood on the dock and watched him until he became part of the waves in the distance.

Walking back toward the beach on the dock, Audra and I stopped several times to admire the way we could look all the way down to the sand in the water. It was beautiful. The second my toes hit the sand, I thought I would go into cardiac arrest. I don't know where she came from, but Chante had descended upon us. "Hello, honeymooners," she said from about ten yards away.

"Hi," Audra, ever the talker, replied. "Look, I didn't mean to offend you the other day." What the fuck was going on? She didn't mean to offend her? When had they talked? I wished I could quickly dig a hole and bury Chante alive in it.

"No, I'm sorry for taking it that way," Chante said. "That's why I came looking for you today." She held out a bottle of red wine. "I brought a peace offering."

"Oh, how sweet." Audra took it and offered Chante a hug. Chante's sinister eyes were digging into mine. "This is my husband . . . James." Audra was making the situation worse.

Chante offered me her cold hand. "Nice to meet you, *James*." I didn't say a word. I just smiled and shook her hand. I wondered what she and Audra had talked about. Why hadn't Audra told me about meeting her? "So what do you lovebirds have planned for the day?"

Audra turned to look at me. "Honey, what are we doing today?"

"Parasailing and fishing," I said sarcastically, since they both knew damn well that we couldn't do anything. I don't know why Chante was playing this stupid game.

"Wow, sounds like fun." Chante kept up her glued-on smile. "Enjoy."

"Oh, we will," I said.

"Thanks so much for the wine," Audra said, trying to excuse us. "We need to go and change."

"No problem," Chante said. "I hope to run into you all later."

I walked past her like it really was the first time I had met her. I was furious and knew that I needed to come clean and let Audra know that she had to stop being so damn naïve. The moment we pulled the sliding door closed, I asked, "Why didn't you tell me you had talked to her?"

"I met her yesterday on the beach," she said, smiling at the bottle of wine. "Isn't this nice?"

"We're not drinking it. Put it in the trash," I said.

"Why?" she asked. "She seems nice. Yesterday when—"

"She knows me," I said. "I know her."

"What do you mean?" She rested the bottle on the counter.

"I met her on the beach last week." I sighed. "But that wasn't my first time meeting her."

"Okay," Audra continued cautiously, "when *was* the first time you met her?"

"Three years ago," I confessed.

"What?" She walked over to me.

"She was one of the girls that Dom paid. I . . . had sex with her." I was a little embarrassed.

"Are you kidding me?" she shouted.

"I wish I was," I said.

"She was paid?" Audra was shocked.

"She was paid that night, yes."

"You slept with a prostitute?"

"Yes." I braced myself. "But we continued to sleep together after that night."

"For how long?" She laughed angrily.

"Off and on for three years, until about three or four months ago."

"So you've been frequenting a prostitute all this time?" Her hands shot up to her head.

"She was only paid once, by Dom," I said. "It grew into something else."

"So she's your girlfriend?"

"No," I answered with a grimace. "Whenever she was in Miami or I was here, we'd kick it sexually, but nothing else. She wanted to be in a relationship, which is the reason I stopped seeing her. It was just a sexual thing."

"Oh, my goodness. She knows that you and I are running?"

"Yes," I said. "That's why I didn't tell you about her. If I don't keep her happy, she could ruin our lives," I said.

"So she was playing me." She was angry. "Asking me a bunch of questions and she knew who I was all along."

"The last time we were together she took it really hard that

I didn't want to move to another level with her. She could really be vindictive and fuck us up big time if she wants to."

"So what do we do?" she asked nervously.

The only thing I could say was, "Keep her happy."

"How?" She pondered. "What exactly does that mean?"

"Well, now that she knows that you are here with me, either we can't stay here or I need to make her happy."

"What exactly do you mean about keeping her happy, by paying her off or something?"

"No, baby." I grabbed her hands. "I'll have to make her think that you are with me just because we're in trouble together."

"I'm supposed to sit back and watch you with another woman?" She pulled her hands away.

"No. I won't be 'with her.' It's just part of the plan for right now," I said. "If I don't do something, she may turn us in. There is a reward on our heads, baby."

"If all y' all did was fuck each other crazy, then that's obviously what makes her happy. So is that what you are going to do?"

I didn't know what in the hell I meant about keeping Chante happy. All I knew was that within an hour we either needed to be off of this island or I needed to be with Chante. Now that she knew I was with a woman, her mind must be in overdrive with drama.

I went for the gusto. "It's for our freedom, Audra."

"So you want to fuck her for our freedom?" she asked with tears coming down her face.

"Listen to me." I grabbed her hands. "Listen to what I'm telling you. Look at me." I waited for her to look at me. "This woman means nothing to me. Yes, we messed around, but she obviously wasn't special enough to win my heart. In a fraction of the time I spent with her you have my heart, mind, and soul tangled up in you. I love *you!*" I pulled her toward me. "I don't know how to explain this, but I'll do anything I can just to have the freedom to be in your arms, baby." I meant every letter of every word I had spoken.

She didn't say anything for a while. I hoped that my words were soaking into all of the insecure areas of her heart. "Fine! So what do we need to do?" she asked.

I kissed her and said, "I just need you to be strong. You have to promise me that you can deal with seeing me interact with her and know that it's all a game."

She sighed. "But how long are we going to have to do this? She lives on this island, so as long as we're here you'll have to keep doing this? When does the 'game' ever end?"

"Just until I figure out where we can go." I tried to keep it real with her. "I don't know how long that will take." I touched her face. "But you have to know that none of it will be real, nothing I do or say with her is anything you need to worry about."

"Whatever!" Her attitude had changed once again. She pulled away and started walking toward the bedroom mumbling, but I distinctly heard her say, "I'm going to have to fuck Dom to stay here anyway, so now we'll be even."

"What?" I yelled from across the room and found myself

in her face before I opened my mouth to say, "What did you just say?"

"Nothing," she lied.

I raised my voice. "What did you say?"

"We'll be even, because the next time Dom comes to town I'm going to have to have sex with him in order to stay here. So there," she spat out at me.

"What are you talking about?" I asked. "He apologized for the fuckin' inappropriate things he said to you. He said that he didn't mean it and that he was drunk. He said the shit to you right in front of me!"

"That was just a portion of what he said to me." She came clean. "Of course he's not going to tell you that he just about fingered me when he grabbed my pussy through my pants and told me that it was his because if it weren't for him I'd be in prison."

"What?" My heart and my mind felt like they were being dragged in different directions. "He fuckin' touched you?"

"Yes." Suddenly she had more to say. "He said that he'd be damned if he would clothe me, feed me, check on my mother, and give me a place to stay without getting something in return. He said that I belonged to him and that he wasn't campaigning for my pussy. The next time he came, either I could give it to him or get the hell out."

"Why didn't you tell me any of this shit?" My vision was blurred and my heart was pumping like it belonged inside of a racehorse. "You told me that he came on to you. Why didn't you tell me about any of this?"

"Because we need a place to stay," she cried. "Where in the hell am I gonna go if I can't stay here? What am I going to do if I'm not with you?" She collapsed into my arms. "I didn't want to tell you while he was still here because I knew how you'd react and he'd probably put us both out or hurt or kill us. I know what kind of guy he is. He frightens me, but at the same time we need him."

"I don't need a muthafucka like that," I said and stepped away from her, forcing her to stand on her own. "He put his hands on you? He threatened you? He told you that you belong to him?" My blood was boiling. "That bastard is supposed to be my brother." I looked at her and saw right past her and onto the wall. I moved away, afraid that if I lashed out to punch the wall I could hurt her too. "The way you said what you said sounds like you would've done it. Is that what you're saying?"

"That's not what I said, Dean," she said. "I didn't know what to do, I—"

I cut her off. "If he had told you last night that you had to have sex with him right then and there or get out, what would you have done?"

She looked away. "I don't know."

"You don't know?" I yelled at her. "What the fuck do you mean you don't know?"

"Well, isn't that the same way you plan on making Chante happy?" she asked. "It's all the same damn thing now, isn't it?" She continued, "It's either we do what everybody wants us to do, go to jail, or give up what we now have and truly start over with nothing. As long as people are helping us they will feel that they have the right to control us." She reached out to me. "Are we going to live in the prison that Chante and Dom are creating for us?"

"Sure sounds like *you* were willing to," I said and yanked my hand away from her. "I'm out!" I was pissed and headed out the door.

JOURNAL ENTRY:

Audra

I waited for an hour by the door for Dean to come back so that I could hold him and be held and have us figure this thing out. An hour came and went . . . nothing. Several hours went by and even the sunset came and went and he still wasn't home. I didn't leave the house. I figured it wouldn't be smart to leave the place completely unmanned, but I was extremely worried about him. I cooked dinner, waited for him to come eat with me, and he didn't. I ate alone and then got ready for bed.

Close to midnight I heard the sliding door open and shut. There was no way I was getting out of bed to greet him. I was the one who should get any type of apology that was supposed to be given. I fixed myself under the sheets to be certain that I looked cute from all angles and waited for him to come in. After thirty minutes I figured he was probably sleeping on the sofa thinking that I wouldn't want him in the bed, but I did.

I huffed, gave up the act, and jumped out of bed. I opened up the door and looked out into the living room to see Dean and Chante on the sofa. She was sitting with her legs draped over his thigh in a very short skirt and he was sliding his hand up and down her calves. There were also two wineglasses on the coffee table and the bottle of wine that he urged me to dispose of.

"Audra!" His eyes nearly jumped out to touch mine when he saw me looking at them. "Sorry, did we wake you?" he asked.

Wow! Was he supposed to call me Audra or Angela? I didn't know what I was supposed to say or do or if I was coming or going. I wanted to slap Chante in the face—that was the only constant thing in my mind. "No." I grimaced and hoped that it wasn't visible. "I was coming out for a snack."

"Hi," Chante said. "You want a snack? You want me to make something?"

"No, thank you. I cooked earlier." Was she serious? I'm sure she thought, as some islanders do, that I was some lazy black American woman who didn't know how to do anything. "Would *you* like something to eat?" I asked sarcastically.

"No, thanks," Chante said. As I walked past them to get to the kitchen, she stood up and followed me. "Dean told me everything, and I just want you to know that you can be comfortable around me. I plan on helping you two as much as I possibly can." She smiled, but why wouldn't she? She had her man, she was ecstatic. "Sorry about what went down on the beach yesterday. Woman to woman, when I thought something was going on between you two it did make me a little jealous. I'm so sorry." She went on with a blatant lie. "But even if you two were together in that way I still would've helped because there is almost nothing that I wouldn't do for Dean."

"Thank you," I said. "That means a lot to the both of us."

"I mean, there is a lot that I can do with that fifty-thousand-dollar reward," she whispered, "but there is a lot more that I can do with him." She giggled. "He's worth way more than that."

I opened the refrigerator and pretended to look for some-thing . . . anything. I grabbed a soda and some cookies. "Want a soda?" I asked.

"No, thanks." She laughed patronizingly. "I'm a nurse. I know what that stuff does to you on the inside."

"Okay." I grabbed two just to make the statement that I didn't give a damn crystal-clear. I snatched a napkin from the rack and started back to the bedroom. "Nice seeing you again, Chante."

"Good night, Audra," Dean said.

Didn't he think that bringing her here warranted more of a conversation or agreement between us? Could I have had some type of advance warning? It took every angel in heaven to hold my tongue from the words I really had for him. "Good night, Dean."

I was beyond upset, and when I closed the bedroom door I opened up the floodgates to my tears and remembered the words Chante said to me on the beach: *"Anything you have, I can*

have within a day, two at the most. Trust me." She was right. It was a
day later and that bitch had my man, even if it's all "pretend,"
as he said. He was out there with her and I was all alone. The
only company I had were my tears, and they couldn't talk
back.

I lay down in the quiet room and knew that under the cur-
rent conditions I would never fall asleep. Hearing Chante's
voice, Dean's laughter, and their banter was hard, but it was
the silence that drove me crazy. That silence meant he was
looking in her eyes, rubbing her legs (again), kissing her. That
silence could mean that she was on her knees in front of him.
Every time there was lengthy quietness, I would sit up and
stare at the door and be just seconds away from busting out
there and saying, "Enough. I can't do this!"

I was on the verge of losing my sanity, so I just kept telling
myself, *It's all a game, it's all a game, it's all just a game that he has to
play.* But was it all a game? Maybe the joke was on me? Maybe
this was truly his plan all along. He knew that he couldn't
leave me in Miami because I would get caught and rat him
out, so he brought me along so that he could be free to be
with his girlfriend of three years? They were probably out
there right now laughing at *my* naïve ass. Perhaps I was just
"something" he had to do to get here to her. Maybe I was *their*
"situation," and they were now plotting about what to do
about me.

In spite of all the crazy things tumbling around in my
mind, somehow I fell asleep. I woke up with Dean's arm
around me. I flung his hand so far off of me that if it wasn't

attached it would be in the other room. "Ouch," he said. "What happened?"

I scooted to the edge of the bed, away from him. "Don't touch me," I said.

"Why not?" he asked in a serious tone.

"Why *not*?" I repeated to make sure that he had just fixed his mouth to ask something so brazenly stupid. "Why not? Because you left here with attitude almighty and came back ten hours later with the woman you were sleeping with. That's why not."

He started talking. "Audra, we talked about that before I left—"

"No!" I stopped him. "You walked out *while* we were talking. Get it right." I turned on the light. "As far as I'm concerned, you can go stay with her. She was your reason for coming here in the first place. I know that the joke is all on me. I can fend for myself."

"What?" He sat up to look directly into my face. "What are you talking about? What do you mean the joke is on you?"

"I mean I've figured it out," I said, and I truly believed what I had been thinking. "You wanted to get here to her. I knew too much and you couldn't leave me back in Miami to snitch, so you brought me along with you. She knew about me all along and knows that you being with me is . . . collateral damage, so to speak." I took a breath. "So now you two are 'pretending' to pretend to be together and all the while trying to plot what to do to or with me."

In the middle of my superb detective work and explanation, Dean couldn't contain his laughter. "Are you serious?" he asked and laughed some more. "Do you think I'm Double-Oh-Seven or some shit?"

"It's not funny, Dean," I said. "And I'm packing my stuff in the morning and just asking for enough money for me to get to another island and stay in a hotel for a week or so. After that I will fend for myself."

"You actually think that you're going to leave me?" he asked with a smile.

"What, you two have plans to drown me or something?" I knew that the things I was saying were over the top, but that didn't mean they couldn't be true. "I refuse to sit here and be made a fool of. You two don't have to pretend anymore. Just be together and let me get on with whatever the hell is left of my life."

"Okay, I know that you've been reading a lot of books lately, but damn, are you serious?" he asked, laughing again so much that his eyes were watering. "That is *New York Times* bestselling book shit right there, babe." He rounded the bed and stood in front of me. "All right, I see that you've had too much time to think today. I'm sorry for running off like that. I went and talked to Larry about something—"

I gasped. "About what I said about Dom?"

"Naw, some other stuff," he said. "I was walking on the beach on my way back here when I met an old man with a small boat on the dock. I went fishing with him. I thought he was only going out for an hour or so, but we got out there and he got excited, so we didn't get back until after sunset."

He went on to explain. "Chante was on the beach again, for whatever reason, so I decided there was no time like the present. Now, I won't lie to you. We sat on the beach for hours talking. I told her about you and me and how I had gotten you involved and couldn't let you go down by yourself." As he went on, it was harder to hear. "She believes that I am attracted to women who look like her, tall and thin, so she believes that nothing sexual has happened between us." He sighed. "I told her that your boyfriend helped us get away and he sends money with Dom whenever he can." He had more to say. "She pushed the issue of her coming up to the house I guess as a last resort to make sure that there was nothing going on between us, so I just brought her up and tried to play it off as best as I could."

"Did you have sex with her?" I had to know.

"Of course not," he answered, as though my question was preposterous. "No, I didn't."

"Well, I *saw* you touching her, so I guess I don't need to ask you that," I said. "But did you kiss her?"

"Yes," he answered honestly, "I did."

"You did?" I had been hoping that he would either lie to me or been man enough to do what he had to do without going there with another woman. "Are you for real?"

He said, "I'm not going to lie to you about anything that happens. I love you and I want you to know everything."

"No. How much you love me should be reflected by you not kissing another woman," I lashed out. "I can't believe you."

"Do you want me to be honest with you or not, Audra?" he asked.

"I want you to be true to me," I said.

"I was." He was frustrated. "When you ask me questions, tell me if you want me to lie before I answer, okay?"

"I don't want you to lie to me," I whined. "But damn, baby."

"I did what I had to do to get her to believe that I am not using her just so she won't turn us in. How could you think that the joke is on you? The joke is on *her*, honey, I promise you that." He pulled me to my feet and held me around the waist. "I have a plan in motion. I can't tell you too much about it just yet, but if everything goes the way I have in mind, we'll be home free soon."

"What is it?" He had to know that I would ask.

"I just need you to play your part in it," he said.

"Okay." I was eager. "What is it?"

"Your part of the plan is just to keep believing in me," he said. "Believe what I tell you. Nothing you see or hear me say to anyone is real unless I am talking to you and we are completely alone." He put my hand over his heart. "Promise me that."

I took a deep breath. "Okay."

"No," he said. "Tell me that you promise."

"I promise to believe in you, baby," I vowed.

"Thank you." He kissed my hand. "In the meantime I'm going fishing with Larry tomorrow afternoon."

"You mean *we* are going fishing with Larry," I said.

"No." He laughed. "I am going fishing with Larry."

We got back in bed. I turned off the lights and allowed him to hold me. "So how come you don't smell like fish if you went fishing with the old guy?" I asked, half joking like women do when they really want to know something.

"Because I took a shower before I crawled into bed to be next to you." He kissed my earlobe. "Would you rather I go roll around in some fish guts and come back?"

"Naw!" I said, giggling. "You might kiss somebody or *something*."

He said, "I have something for *you* to kiss."

"I bet you do," I said.

"So you want to?"

I blushed. "Are you asking me to suck your dick?"

"Yes!" He then asked jokingly, "Is that a problem?"

"Yes," I replied. "Sometimes a woman needs to be told, not asked." For some reason I really got off on that, but that's a whole other story.

"I remember that you like a little bullying," he said.

"Yeah," I confessed, "*but* only in the bedroom."

"Mmm, so you want me to be your bedroom bully, huh?"

I was feeling freakish all of a sudden. "Yeah."

He wrestled with his pants until they were off. "Suck my dick," he demanded as he sat up with his back against the headboard and dragged me over to him, positioning me between his legs. "Suck this dick until I come on those pretty lips of yours."

"Which lips?" I asked.

"No questions!" He played the role well. "Get that dick in your mouth."

Some psychiatrists would probably say that I have unresolved or suppressed sexual issues, but that's not so. I'm not traumatized by anything from my childhood. I've just always had this thing for being told or somewhat made to perform sexual acts. Don't get me wrong. I'm sure if I was truly being forced to do something, I wouldn't find it appealing, but I loved to role-play, be teased to the extreme, or be forced. The ultimate was the first time Dean and I had sex . . . the consensual rape. There will never be anything as sexy as that to me.

"Ooooh yes, Dean." I took his dick into my mouth and sucked and stroked him just the way I knew he liked it. I loved the smell, feel, and look of his dick, and that just made me go even wilder and work harder to get him all the way in. "Mmmm," I groaned, and in a second had that dick so far in my mouth that if he wanted to see the tip of it again he'd have to cross over; his shit was in another dimension. I was trying to swallow it, and all of this made my pussy water like Miami's sky in the spring.

"Yeah, suck it, baby." He put his hand in back of my head, encouraging me to continue to take him in like that again and again. "Just like that, until I come." He made my lips hit his shaft each and every time I went down. It was pretty intense, my eyes were watering, my mouth felt numb and like it would remain stuck in the open position for days, but I was sucking up some dick and my man loved it. It got to a point where he couldn't even talk nasty to me the way I required.

All he could do was squirm and groan. The last time I went down he squealed and suddenly expelled a gush of come into my mouth. I swallowed and followed up by licking the rest of it from his region, leaving him completely dry.

"Damn, girl," he said, totally spent like he had done the work and not me. "Where did that come from?"

"That's what happens when you bully me," I said.

"Well, this is now a dictatorship, and I'm in charge at all times," he joked.

"Yes, sir," I said as I rolled out of bed to brush my teeth.

When I returned he was knocked out, so I just cuddled up next to him, draped his hand over me, and felt safe as long as he was around.

JOURNAL ENTRY:

Dean

For the moment, everything I had told Audra about Chante was true, but I couldn't tell her about the plan I had already set in motion, because it truly didn't include her and I knew that it would break her heart. I had to leave her behind. I had weighed all of my options and it was just the smart thing to do. It had to happen and had to happen quickly. This couldn't be postponed a month, a week, or even a day . . . It meant freedom and it meant now.

"You ready?" Larry said as I opened the door for him.

"Yeah," I whispered as I looked at the bedroom door. Audra was getting dressed. I gave Larry the keep-it-down gesture.

"Oh, sorry," he said. "Dom is on his way back. He should be here any minute now."

"Cool." I nodded my head in approval.

Larry looked around. "Where is your stuff?" he asked.

"I packed up as much as I could while she was sleeping."

I kept my voice down. "I threw my bag out on the beach earlier."

"What about the money?" Larry inquired. "Where is the money?"

"Out there in my bag," I said. "I left about five grand for Audra." I felt terrible about the decision I was about to make.

Larry looked like he didn't give a damn. "Where is Chante?"

"She's going to meet us on the docks at noon." I looked at my watch, it was already after ten.

"Good morning, Larry!" Audra came out looking like a ray of sunshine, literally in the loudest yellow sundress I had ever seen. She looked radiant.

"Mornin', Audra." Larry greeted her with a hug and a kiss on the cheek. "How you doin'?"

She winked at me before she answered. "A little drained, but wonderful, couldn't be better. Would either of you like a glass of orange juice?"

"Yes. Heavy sugar, light cream," Larry joked.

She was clueless as to what was really happening. "So how long are you guys going to be out there fishing?" she asked from the kitchen.

"Probably for a while," I answered before Larry could. "So make sure that you lock up when we go."

"Are you going with the old guy you went with yesterday?" she asked as she opened the orange juice.

"No," I replied.

"We're going with Dom." Larry thought he was helping me.

"Dom?" Audra turned to look at me and nearly spilled the juice on the counter. "Dom is here?"

"He's on his way back," I said. "He's bringing the yacht this time so that we can fish and chill a little."

Her eyes were full of disappointment, and I knew that if Larry wasn't there she'd say something about me going out to chill with the guy whose neck I'd wanted to rip off just a day before. She said nothing, so I assume she bought into what I had told her about going along with and believing in what I was doing or saying to her even if it didn't seem right.

We all sat around and talked until Dom arrived. "What's up?" he said as he yanked opened the sliding door with a vengeance. "Is that your bag out there?" he asked.

"Yeah," I said shamefacedly. I was trying to hide that from Audra.

"What bag?" she mouthed to me, but I pretended not to see her.

"I saw Chante on the beach with her bags. I told her to get on the boat, so let's roll, guys," Dom said. I wondered if he was purposely revealing information he knew I didn't want divulged. "Let's get this party started!"

Audra stood up with her hands on her hips and stopped short of rolling her eyes at me. She didn't say a word, just went to the bedroom. I knew what that meant—she wanted me in there too.

"You got everything?" Larry questioned Dom.

"Let's go. We have to move fast," Dom said with a crooked smile.

"All right," I said. "Give me a minute to say good-bye."

Dom and Larry gathered their things and headed out the door. When Audra heard the door slam, she probably assumed I left and came running out. "What the hell is going on?" she asked me.

"I told you. We're going fishing."

"With Chante?" she asked. "Why in the hell is she going, and why are most of your things gone? There is hardly any money in the safe." Tears slithered down her cheeks.

"It's not what it looks like," I lied.

"Then tell me what's going on," she insisted.

I wanted to tell her the truth, but I wasn't man enough to. "I can't, baby." I touched her face. "I'm sorry."

"Where are you really going?" she asked. "Are you coming back?"

I couldn't stick around. She'd have to get over it—this was a move I had to make. I had to leave her behind. I had to think smart, not with my heart. I could never do what needed to be done with her by my side. "I have to go, Audra." I kissed her on the forehead as I had done plenty of times before, but this time it felt like I was leaving my soul behind. "I love you!"

"No!" she cried. "Don't tell me that," she stuttered and tried holding on to me. "Don't tell me that unless you tell me why you're taking your clothes and money."

"Remember what I told you about not believing what you see or hear, baby, remember that?" I whispered to her.

"Yeah, but this is different. You have bags. Chante has bags.

You've taken our money and you're getting on a boat with Dom. It's not 'what it looks like.' Everything is *done*. It is what it is," she yelled through her tears. "At least be man enough to tell me what you're doing. Don't just leave me like this."

"I can't." The drama was too much for me. I was losing focus. I pulled away from her. "Please lock up when I leave." I walked off and she followed me. "Don't come outside," I begged her. "Just let me go," I looked into her sad eyes, "Just let me go."

And she did. She was in shock, in pain, in turmoil, but she let me go. She didn't say another word as I closed the door. I just heard her crying. I watched her fall to her knees and reach out to me.

I ran down to the beach to the dock, helped Larry untie the boat, and jumped onto the yacht. I had been on it countless times before and had even taken the helm several times, but this time was different; it would be all business, no pleasure. Chante greeted me on the stern with a hug and a huge kiss. I hoped that Audra wasn't looking. That would be a devastating final blow to her.

"Hi, honey!" she said. "I can't believe that we're doing this."

"I can't believe that you *wanted* to do this," I responded.

"I told you . . ." She smiled. "I'd do anything for you."

I looked back at the house. "You know that being with me makes you a criminal, right?"

"Yep," she said. "But when we make it to Haiti everything will be good, right?"

"It should be," I said, "but who knows."

To get my mind off of other things, I told Dom that I would man the helm as long as he helped me to navigate. About an hour into our trip, Larry, leaving Chante in the other section, joined us and said, "Let's stop here."

"Yeah," Dom said. "Let's have some cocktails." He winked at me.

We all walked into the lounge area of the boat. Larry went to the bar to make us drinks.

"Why are we stopping?" she asked. "Isn't it best to keep going? We'll get there faster?"

"I'm in no rush," Dom said. "Are you?"

"No, no." She fumbled over her words. "I'm not rushing you."

"I'm taking it slow," Dom said. "Speaking of slow . . . how about some slow head from you right now?"

"What?" She seemed confused.

"What?" Dom mocked her and then translated blatantly, "Come suck my dick."

She looked over at me. "What?"

"What are you looking at him for?" he asked. "This is *my* boat."

"But I'm *with* him," she said. "Plus, I don't do that any-more."

"C'mon, you sucked my dick last month and I beat that pussy to death just a couple weeks ago." Dom laughed. "No worries, though, this will be your last time," he said. "You've gotten better over the years, plenty of practice on my boys.

You have my shit hard right now." Dom grabbed his dick through his pants. "Come suck this dick."

"I don't want to," Chante said. "I didn't think I was here for that." She looked over at me. "Dean, tell him."

"Relax," Dom said. "I'm kidding." Right then Larry came in with drinks for everyone. Michelob Ultras for Dom and me, a Heineken for himself, and a mixed drink for the lady. Minutes into our drinks and making small talk, Chante asked, "Is the air-conditioning on?"

"Why?" Dom asked.

"I'm feeling hot," she said, looking troubled. She put her hand over her heart. "I think I'm getting seasick or something."

"What?" Dom chuckled. "What are you feeling?"

"Dizzy." Chante looked over at me. "I'm very dizzy."

"You're not seasick. I think you might have that disease that's killing people these days," Dom said. "I think its called snitchitis."

"What is that?" She started breathing heavily.

"Snitchitis? You were going to snitch him out if he didn't agree to be with you, that's what it is." Dom stood up. "If he goes down, I go down! Do you think that I'm going to let you, a fifty-cent whore, bring down me and my fuckin' family? "Hell no," he yelled.

"Something is wrong with me." She looked at me and panicked. Soon she was struggling to breathe. "Something was in my drink."

"Did you put something in her drink?" I asked Dom.

"Yep, hydrogen cyanide," he answered.

Chante screamed and tried to stand but fell to the floor. I tried to help her. Her body was shaking, and before her eyes began to roll back I could tell that she heard him and knew what was about to happen to her—after all, she was a nurse.

This wasn't in my plan. "Dom, I thought we were just going to scare her, threaten her. Pay her off. What the fuck did you do?" I was staring at him.

"Fuck that," Dom yelled. "My family don't fuckin' threaten people. We don't make threats. We deliver. This bitch was making threats and she's getting what she deserved."

Chante went into convulsions and her body started trembling. There was nothing I could do for her. "Damn, Dom." I looked down at Chante and knew that I didn't want the kind of freedom she was about to receive. I had to man up and get the job done.

"What the fuck are you upset about?" Dom asked.

"Nothing." I played it off. "That shit just shocked me." I looked down at Chante. "You could've told me about that."

"We're going to dump her. We're the only people who know where she is. She thought she was going to Haiti . . . well, she still is." He laughed. "If I didn't do this she was going to talk, no doubt, trust me."

Larry had fixed the drink, but he hadn't said a word during the whole ordeal. I had heard about things Dom had done to people, but I never witnessed it. This was a part of him that I had never seen. I felt like I didn't know this guy at all.

"Larry, there are some blocks and rope down below," Dom said, and Larry, the henchman, disappeared.

It was now do-or-die time. I was scared. I knew if Dom had even a hint of my plan, I'd be dead. "Do you have a gun?" I asked him.

"Yeah," he answered. "Up front in the cabinet. Why?"

"I do too." I pulled my Glock from the waist of my pants and pointed it toward him.

"What?" He was laughing but confused. "What are you doing?"

"You won't let me live long, Dom. Soon I'll be bringing too much heat to you. That's why you want to take me to Colombia," I said.

"What the fuck are you doing?"

"I'm trying to live," I told him.

"Then live, bitch, but get that shit out of my face." He moved toward me. "Gimme that fuckin'—." BAM! My finger moving backward was a reflex. In stepping back from him, the gun fired. The bullet dug into Dom's head, and he dropped to his knees and then forward onto his face. Just seconds later Larry rushed in.

"What was that?" He looked down at Dom. "What the fuck?" He looked over at me. I pointed the gun at him and this time I pulled the trigger on purpose. I shot Larry twice in the chest. I was exhausted. My body felt drained. The gun fell from my hand to the ground.

I trembled. Three bodies, three *dead* bodies were at my feet. I wasn't a thug, a gangster, or a hardened criminal. I had seen

dead people only in coffins. I was freaked out. I threw up over
and over again and didn't move for an hour. I couldn't believe
how many lives had been taken so I could make a clean break.
This didn't feel like an ending. It felt like the beginning of a
nightmare.

When Audra told me about what Dom had done and said
to her, I questioned and came to doubt his love and respect for
me. So that, coupled with a few things Larry unconsciously
let slip, made me realize that Dom wasn't who I thought he
was. In order for me to stay in the house, he was going to use
me in some deal with a Colombian gang he had problems
with. If I survived that, his intentions were to kill me before I
started bringing heat to his family. I had to get him, before he
got me. It was his life or mine.

Larry would have let Dom's family know that Dom was
missing. I had brought Chante along to help me get rid of both
of them. But eventually my plan was somehow to get rid of
her too, because if she couldn't have me, she would damn sure
turn on me.

Chante had been under the impression that I was leaving
Bimini and going to Haiti with her on my arm in search of
freedom. Dom and Larry knew the story I had concocted for
Chante, but they truly thought I simply wanted to get her
into the middle of the ocean to threaten her about not going
to the police and pay her off. Obviously, they had plans of
their own.

I tied their bodies to cinder blocks and tossed them off the
boat, miles apart from one another, like rag dolls. It was very

haunting. The water was so clear it took awhile for each of them to disappear from my view to the bottom. It was something I never expected to experience in my lifetime. How had it come to this? I had just killed a man I loved like a brother, someone who had become a friend, and watched a woman I was fond of die partially in my arms. Now what?

JOURNAL ENTRY:

Audra

I was heartbroken, paranoid, scared, lonely—
everything all at once. Since day one I was scared
about being caught, paranoid about not being vigilant
enough, and now for the past two days brokenhearted. Dean
was gone. Fishing for two days? I guess he saw a neon light
that read "stupid" right on my forehead. He found me the
perfect person to drag to Bimini to keep me quiet just long
enough to hatch a plan and run away with his *real* woman.

The moment Chante greeted him with a hug and kiss, I
knew it would be a cold day in hell before I saw him again.
Nothing about the way his arms welcomed her around the
waist implied that he was acting. Dom and Larry escorted the
lovely couple to another safe tropical haven.

There was no way I was going to make it on my own. He'd
left about five grand, but where could that take me? Where
would I go? And how long would it be before Dom returned

and asked me to put out or get out? My only choice seemed to be hopping on a plane to Miami, being intercepted by customs and turned over to the police. Maybe I could convince them that I had been a hostage all along. Perhaps I could make an interrogation room filled with street-smart cops believe I was still the victim I started out as. I was deserving of freedom. My only crime was falling in love.

I had lost a very real game of truth, lies, murder, and love. I didn't qualify to put my initials among the high scores. I just played the game and lost. For two days I stayed locked up in the house, but on the third day I couldn't take it anymore. My spirits were way down. I opened the sliding door and enjoyed the ocean air on my face. I stepped out into the breeze and minutes later found myself on the beach. Another sunset. It was beautiful, absolutely stunning. Boats were coming and going in the distance, and I wished I was on one of them. Whenever I thought of turning myself in, I thought of the water, the sunrises and sunsets, that I would be separated from and the thoughts would quickly go away.

I stood arms akimbo in knee-high water hoping that the tide would take with it all of my problems and stresses. But they just kept floating around and around me, taunting my ankles like guppies. I watched a boat slowly come in. It started out about a mile away, and when it was just seventy-five yards away, it started to look familiar. Is that Dom's boat? I wondered. I tried to look away, but it got closer and closer and then slowly pulled up to the dock. It was a yacht, but I had seen Dom's boat only very briefly from the back.

The name on the boat was *Spicy Meat Balls!* Now I was certain it was Dom's. When the yacht was adjacent to the dock, I knew that in seconds someone had to come out to tie it up. I waited patiently. When the door opened and a bag flew out, I took a deep breath and watched in complete awe as Dean stepped into the rapidly sinking sunlight. My heart dropped into my toes and bounced back into my chest just in time for me to smile back at him. I stepped out of the water and walked to the dock's beach end. He tied up the boat, and I dreaded the moment Chante would walk off. He'd probably embrace or kiss her, and that would truly send me into a realm of anger I had yet begun to explore.

He started down the dock and I moved toward him. I wanted to run, but I didn't know if Chante was watching. I collapsed into his arms and he dropped his bag and held me around the waist and rubbed my back. He kissed the top of my head over and over again, then brought his lips down to mine for a quick peck. I kissed him on his chest, through his shirt, several times before his body odor slapped me square in the face. Though he had on different clothing than he left in, Dean smelled like garbage that was neglected by the roadside on the hottest day of summer.

"I didn't think you were coming back," I cried.

We stood there for about five minutes holding, kissing, and breathing each other in. "I didn't think you were coming back." I had to say it again.

"I know," he replied.

"Where is everyone?" I inquired.

He let go of me and grabbed his bag. "I dropped 'em off."

"Dropped 'em off?" I was perplexed. "Where?"

He didn't say another word until we were in the house. He threw himself on the bed. "I need a warm bath."

"You need *any* kind of bath," I joked and hovered over him. "You smell like an egg-salad sandwich after it leaves the body."

He didn't laugh or smile. He simply asked, "Will you run some water for me?"

"What's wrong?" I was taken aback by how downtrodden he looked and sounded.

He took a deep breath. "We need to get away from here."

"Why?" I asked. "Did Dom say something?"

"Just run the water, please." He sounded upset. "I need to sit and think."

I went into the bathroom and ran the water as he just about demanded of me. I added a few drops of bubble bath and called out to him, "The water is ready."

He entered the bathroom, and recognizing my standoffish atitude, he touched my shoulder. "I'm sorry if I seem a little different." He looked at me strangely. "There is a lot on my mind." He looked like he wanted to cry. "Just give me a moment alone, and I promise we'll talk when I'm done."

I closed the door, went into the kitchen to make him a quick ham sandwich, and couldn't help speculating on what he was so down about. Of course I was glad he was back, but two days had gone by. I was supposed to be the one acting mad. He had to know that I would have a million and one

questions. I figured I could deal with him telling me anything . . . except that he had sex with Chante. *That* I couldn't
recover from.

I took a beer and the sandwich into the bathroom and
found him in the tub staring up at the ceiling. "Here you go,
baby." I handed him the plate and put the beer on the edge of
the tub.

"Anything else I can do for you?" I was trying hard to not
be a pain, to let him relax, but my mind was fishing for information.

"Naw." He bit into the sandwich.

I gave up. "Okay," I said and just waited on the bed.

An hour later he emerged and hit me with a one-two-three
punch. "Chante, Dom, and Larry are dead," he said as calmly
as if he had just said, "Chante, Dom, and Larry are coming for
dinner."

"What happened?"

"Everything happened," he said.

"How did you survive? Did something happen to the
boat?" Then I remembered that the boat was fine. I was confused and scared. "Did they drown?"

"It's all fucked up," he said, and I saw the tears form, but he
didn't allow them to fall. "I can't believe it."

I moved in to comfort him, "What happened, honey?"

His face trembled; he couldn't hold back the tears anymore.
"Dom . . . Dom poisoned Chante," he said. "I didn't know he

was going to do it. We were supposed to be taking her out there to scare her into keeping her mouth shut. She thought that she and I were running off to Haiti, but we were taking her out there to pay her off and threaten her a little. But Dom took it to the next level."

"He poisoned her . . . killed her?" I asked.

He nodded.

Dean was silent for a while, then he told me the whole story.

"Oh, my God." I stared at him. "You killed Dom and Larry?"

"Yeah," he said. "In all honesty, that was the plan when I left here—"

"What about Chante?" I asked. "Where you going to kill her too?"

He looked away. "Eventually." His honesty was overwhelming. "But I was going to let her think that she was helping me. That's why I took her and not you: I didn't want to risk anything happening to you. I didn't even know if I would make it out alive." He could tell that I was frightened of him. "I was surprised to see you by the docks."

"Why?" I asked.

"Because of the note I left you in the journal." From the look on my face he realized I hadn't seen the note. "In it I told you that if I wasn't back by sunset to take the money and leave." He shook his head. "Things went down pretty quickly, but I got lost on the way back. My mind was so fucked up I couldn't tell east from west, north from south. It took me a whole day to figure out how to read the compass right, and by then I was halfway to nowhere."

"I'm glad I didn't see that note," I said. "I wouldn't want to be anywhere else, or with anyone else. But I'm freaked out about this whole thing; it hasn't solved any of our problems. Do you realize that you *killed* two people?"

"I know." He offered me his hand as an olive branch. "Audra, I'm not an animal . . . please don't think of me like that. I had to do what I did in order for us to live. At first I didn't think I would be able to follow through with it, but when I saw Chante die, I imagined that Dom would do the same or worse to you, and I knew I had to stop him."

"So what do we do now?" I asked.

"We get in that boat, get some gas, and island-hop until we find somewhere to be," he said.

"We are wanted," I reminded him. "We can't move aimlessly through any country. We are fugitives from justice."

"Well, we can't just sit here and wait for the Bianchi family to come knocking either," Dean stated. "And people here are going to start wondering where Larry is, or why Chante hasn't shown up for work. We have to get off of the island."

"What if there is a tracking device or something on the boat and his family or the police find us regardless of where we are?" I asked.

"Well, Dom had over a half a million dollars on the boat—it's ours now. Hell, we can buy another boat. But we have to get off of this island—soon," he urged me.

"Okay," I conceded. "I'll start packing."

As I got my things together, we discussed what we would do. We didn't go to bed until after three.

The next morning he loaded our things and everything that was edible onto the boat. I hated the idea of leaving the house. I felt safe there. But as Dean said, sooner or later Dom's family would be all over it and we shouldn't be anyhere around. When I got on the boat, I thought of only one thing: Where did these people die? He showed me. Dean had done a remarkable job cleaning up after the incident. There was no blood or sign that anything had gone down. But still, I was very spooked out about being on a boat where three people had died violent deaths. I imagined that their spirits were still lurking around and would haunt us until we pissed our pants, but this comes from a woman who can't read a Stephen King novel or watch a horror flick without losing a week of sleep.

In hats and shades, we went around to the other side of the island to fill the gas tank. Dean actually had me approach the gas guys and pay them. He was afraid they would recognize him from his times there with Dom. I was careful not to talk too much or ask any questions.

When we pulled off into the big blue sea there was an eerie calm, not just of the waters but in our lives. We seemed normal for the first time since we'd met. He stood at the wooden helm and I came up behind him, wrapped my arms around his waist, and kissed his back. "Where to, Captain?" I teased.

"Everywhere!" he answered with a chuckle. "Everywhere and nowhere all at once."

"You need help navigating?" I asked.

"I'm not all that nautical," he admitted. "I might need a little guidance. The ocean is nothing to be lost in, there are no road signs."

I played around with a couple of things until the GPS screen popped up. It was a touch screen: you touch the region you want to go to, select an island, and it will tell you what you need to do to get there, just like in a car. He had been on the boat lost for two days and just two minutes in, I had clicked a button and saved the world. Men!

We were in no real rush, so we took our time getting to the Bahamian island of Mayaguana. From what we read about the island on the GPS, it was the least developed and most secluded island in the Bahamas. It seemed ideal for us. Thanks to Larry's bogus passport collection and IDs on the boat we were able to clear customs and dock on the island. Because it was so small and remote, we dared to walk around. We hardly saw anyone. The beaches seemed untouched, the birds were all of the colors of the rainbow, and the air was crisp. Something I read said that about three hundred people lived on the island. What was this, the Mayberry of the Caribbean? No one here could possibly know who we were. I would even dare to say that no one here had a television set. It was that type of place. There was one hotel, the Baycaner Beach Resort, and we checked into it.

"Wow!" I looked out the window and directly onto the beach. "Who wouldn't want to live here?"

Dean walked up behind me and squeezed by butt. "Who wouldn't want to live *here*?"

"In my ass?" I turned around.

He laughed. "Yep!"

"Are you into anal sex?" I normally asked every man I dated this question just so that he'd know off the top that he wouldn't be getting it from me.

"Define 'into' it?" he asked.

"Oh, Lord." I giggled. "That means you're *into* it."

"I've done it," he said, shrugging his shoulders. "It's no big deal."

"You've done it?" I decided to carry on jokingly. "Did you give or receive?"

"What?" He was appalled. "I definitely wasn't on the receiving end . . . hell no."

"I was just kidding," I said. "So what is it about anal sex that men like so much?" Before he could answer I went on, "Why would you want to pass up a nice, fat, juicy pussy to get in a dried-up, stinky booty hole?"

"Dried-up, stinky booty hole?" He laughed. "Because it's tight." He kept it real. "It's tight, and with a rubber and the right lubrication it is *very* enjoyable. But it's not for everyone, and not something I'd want to do every day."

"Wow, Dean, I'm surprised to learn that you are such an anal aficionado." I laughed and really didn't know what to make of his revelation. I had always thought it was disgusting and, most important, that too much of it will cause your ass to start looking wide, and that was the last thing I needed. "Well, I'm sorry to inform you, but I don't take it up the rear, never have and never will."

"Oh, you will," he joked as he slapped me on the butt. "I'm gonna get it while you're sleeping."

"Sure! Make it on a night when I've had some sort of beans." I giggled. "It'll be quite memorable for you."

"That's sick." He made a face that quickly turned into a smile. "How about the other hole? Is that store closed for the day?"

"What other hole?" I played the dumb-blonde role.

He rubbed me through my pants. "This one."

"Hmmm . . ." I pretended to have to think, then decided to play hard to get. "Yeah, the store is closed. The owner lost the key, and that's the only way in."

"Mmmm." He chuckled. "Is that right?"

"Yeah." I stepped away from him. "Sorry," I said with a smile and a wink.

"Don't be." He gently pushed me in the direction of the bed, and when my calves were against it he sat me down and pressed me backward until I was lying on my back. "I think I have the key to open up your business."

"Really?" I asked as he pulled down my pants to reveal that I wasn't wearing any undies.

"Ooooh." He looked at my heaving bare vagina and said, "Yeah, I'm certain I have the key that'll open that lock." He touched my lock with his finger, rubbing it slowly until it was so moist that it started making noises. "You ready for me to try the lock?"

"Yeah." I was already somewhere between ecstasy and bliss. "Put your key into my keyhole and let's see if it'll turn."

"If you insist," he said teasingly as he hopped off the bed and stripped, revealing his solid, sharp skeleton key. He stroked his key a few times as he stared between my legs. "Open up wide, baby," he instructed, and I complied.

He teased my lock with his key. His key rubbed against my lock, pressed up on it, and even partially inserted and pulled out quickly. He had oiled the lock up so much that the next time he fell into it he wasn't man enough to leave it. I had *him* on lock now. Ha-ha-ha! He continued to try the lock over and over and over again, and we both knew it was the right key. He put one of my legs up onto his shoulder and turned the key in the lock. That's when he opened up the store—the lights went on, the cash register opened, and the "Come in, we're open" sign was swinging in the window.

"Damn," I said softly.

"Say it again." He was cocky with it.

And I got cocky back. "*Make* me say it again."

He lifted my leg higher and plunged so deep into my pussy that I started asking him to stop. It was that pleasure-pain combination I love, but I knew I was going to be walking funny for at least two days. "Stop, baby."

"No."

"Oooh, shit," I yelled as he began slinging faster and faster. "Dean!"

"Yes, baby?"

"Stop. You're going to make me come and scream."

"That's the whole point, Audra." He didn't miss a beat. "Scream. I love it when you get loud. Scream for Big Daddy."

He worked me onto my stomach. I backed it up as much I could, until his dick became overwhelmingly good. "Ooooooh," I shouted, and for the next several minutes I wailed incoherently as my juices spewed onto him and my body was continually pounded from the back. I came so hard that the spurt pushed Dean out of me.

"Wow, baby," he said as he worked his way back into my panting, tired, yet juicy body.

I couldn't talk, I couldn't move. I just let him have what was left of me. I was done. I raised the white flag, surrendering to my master. He had won the battle, the war, the land . . . Whatever we were fighting for, it was his. Dean was getting it and didn't need me to give back; he was taking it and I was letting him. Soon he grew warm within me and his milk filled my internal cup.

JOURNAL ENTRY:

Dean

We stayed in Mayaguana for two days, then headed back out to sea. With the fake passports and IDs I knew that we could gain access wherever we wanted, but I was wary of how long we'd be able to do it. I decided we should just settle down, somewhere. As soon as Dom was announced missing, his boat would be too. We would leave the boat in the Dominican Republic, switch to different IDs, and then quickly fly to France.

"God, I wish we were just doing this for fun," Audra said as we looked at the tropical paradise and waved good-bye to it. "I can imagine how sweet it would be if we weren't on the run."

"Well, my dear," I chimed in, "if we weren't in this situation, we couldn't afford any of this." I laughed.

She cuddled up to me and helped me turn the wheel. She had already done her magic on the GPS, setting our course for the Dominican Republic. Without her, we would be somewhere in the Bermuda Triangle. However, if we could ping a satellite for directions, then it was pinging us for a location, and that meant we could be located. But how else were we going to find where we were going? Another reason I wanted to get rid of the boat—fast.

It was a beautiful day. The sun was blazing and the crystal-clear waters were calm. It was perfect, almost too good to be true, and you know what they say about things that seem too good to be true. I don't know if it was just paranoia, but I expected something to go wrong before sundown, just had that feeling in my gut. But I didn't want to be a killjoy, so I didn't mention it to Audra. I just held on tight to the paradise outside the window and even tighter to the paradise we shared together. In the midst of the turmoil in my mind, I looked over at her and thanked God for putting her in my life, regardless of the situation. I was so grateful to have her at my side.

Later in the day we had sandwiches and iced tea, and danced to every R & B song the radio picked up. As the sun was ready to set, I figured we should call it a day and start again in the morning. I dropped the anchor and turned off the engine. We chilled together in the living room area for a minute and then Audra had an idea. "Let's have tequila sunrises as we watch the sunset."

"Sounds good, but you know how I feel about tequila, baby." I frowned. "I don't see how you drink that gasoline."

She laughed. "Fine, I'll make me one. What should I make for you?"

"You don't have to make anything for me," I said. "I'm fine."

"I don't want to drink alone," Audra whined. "Plus, we're supposed to toast the sunset together."

"Fine," I conceded. "Make me anything that doesn't have tequila in it."

"Cool," she said and disappeared behind the bar and started shaking and stirring up stuff.

I leaned back onto the sofa and watched the sky turn pink, orange, and light purple, a color combination that couldn't look good anywhere else but in the sky. Suddenly I felt a tingle on the left side of my chest. It felt good. I took it to mean that my heart was smiling and I knew that somewhere Destiny was looking up at the sky thinking about me and feeling my love wrapped up in hues of pink, orange, and purple. If I had one wish it would be to be with her. Suddenly one of the last things I said to her came to mind: *"It may not be tomorrow, next week, or next year, but you will see me again. Just be patient and know that this is not the way I want it, but this is the way that things have to be for right now."* When I said it, I believed it, but somehow now I felt like I had lied to my baby, and it broke my heart. I thought about the moment I let her hand go, and then the tears began flowing. I prayed she was watching the sunset.

"Hey, what's wrong, baby?" Audra asked in shock, returning with two glasses and seeing her man broken down. She rested the drinks on the coffee table.

I wiped my eyes. "Destiny," I said.

"Aw, baby, I'm sorry." She sat next to me with her hand on my thigh. "You missing her?"

"Like crazy," I admitted. "The most I've been without her was a week, and now it's been almost two months. I'm starting to feel like I'll never see her again."

"What?" she exclaimed. "Why would you say that?"

"C'mon, Audra. You think we'll ever see the United States again and live to tell about it?"

She was trying to ease my pain. "Maybe we can fly her to France when we get settled."

"How? Don't you think the FBI will be in the seat behind her on the plane?"

"Dean, we'll find a way, I promise you." She kissed me on the cheek. "I love you!"

I smiled at her because I truly believed that she did. She too made my heart smile. "I love you too."

We did a cheers. "To the sunset," she said.

"To the sunset," I repeated as our glasses kissed. I didn't put the glass to my mouth. The scene was so beautiful that I didn't want to taint it with anything. I just held her in my arms until the sun was done.

We both took a deep breath and then she broke the silence. "I'm going to take a shower, honey."

"Okay," I said. "Leave the water on for me." The shower wasn't big enough for both of us and the slow trickle of water definitely couldn't be shared.

I waited until she was in the shower for a minute to start drinking, and though it was a little bitter it wasn't anything to complain about. I did ask her just to mix me up something, anything without tequila. Halfway through the glass I was feeling weird, not drunk but hot, light-headed, and short of breath. My heart started beating triple time, and I couldn't stand up. "Audra," I called with all my might, but it came out as a whisper. "Audra," I whispered again. I gathered all of my strength and fought to stand up, rested the glass on the table, then took two steps and fell flat onto my face. "Audra!"

JOURNAL ENTRY:

Audra

Baby, I'm out, the water is on for you," I called out to Dean. I plopped down on the bed and was rubbing lotion on my legs when I saw a boat in the distance through the porthole. It seemed to be moving in our direction. "Dean," I panicked because we hadn't encountered many boats before. "Dean," I called again, and when I got no answer and didn't hear him moving toward me, I walked into the living room area. I saw him facedown on the floor. "Dean!"

I knelt down and rolled him onto his side and then onto his back. "Baby?" I didn't know what had happened. I looked around the room and no one else was there; everything was just as I left it. "Dean, talk to me."

He was moving his mouth but not words came out. I pulled him up onto the love seat. His breathing was labored and he looked like he'd pass out at any second. "What's wrong, baby?" I was crying. "Talk to me. What happened?"

His eyes started rolling back into his head, but I could tell he was fighting it. They fell into place again and his hand slowly rose and he pointed at the coffee table. He coughed a bit and spit up on himself, but it helped him get his words out. "Poison," he said, pointing at his drink. "Dom gave to Chante."

"What? What do you mean?"

"Was in a"—he coughed—"a bottle behind the bar."

"Oh, my God." I started to tremble. "No, no, Dean." I ran to the refrigerator and grabbed the gallon bottle of water. "Open your mouth, you need to drink some water," I yelled at him. "Open your mouth, Dean." He was limp and not responding, but his eyes were open and moving. "Dean . . ." My tears were all over his face. I tried pouring the water into his mouth, but it just drained out, and when he did take a little in it seemed to be choking him. I couldn't let him die. "I'm going to call for help on the radio," I cried.

I then remembered the boat I had seen; I looked out the bigger window and still saw it coming. The lights were blaring and now it was just about fifty yards away. I was excited and hoped that someone would be able to help us. "Baby, there is a boat right there. I'm gonna get their attention."

He just stared at me with his chest barely rising and falling. "Dean, don't you die," I instructed him and kept my eye on the boat. I didn't want to leave him alone until the boat was close enough to hear me yelling from the stern. It looked like a yacht, but it was coming fast like a speedboat. It was white, with an orange stripe on the side. "Dean, breathe, baby, breathe." I looked into his eyes. "I love you!" A tear ran down his right cheek, and I knew that it was his response to me.

When I looked out of the window again, the words U.S. COAST GUARD slapped me dead in the face. I looked at Dean for guidance; he would have to tell me what to do. "Baby, it's the Coast Guard," I said, sobbing.

"Dean Tyson, we know that you are aboard this vessel," a voice on a loudspeaker informed us. "We are asking that you and any passengers aboard come out onto the stern with your hands in the air."

"Dean," I yelled at him, weeping, "tell me what to do."

He moved his mouth and weakly pulled my head to his ear. "Go out with your hands up," he said and struggled to continue. "Tell them that you poisoned me as self-defense because I had been hurting you. Tell them I killed everybody else and was about to kill you. Tell them, so that you can be free." He finished, "I'm about to be free too, so don't you worry about me."

"No, Dean," I said. "They can save you, they have medical supplies."

"No." He shook his head. "No."

"Baby, no." My heart was racing. "Let them help you."

"No," he said adamantly in his whisper. "This is freedom for me."

"Well, for me too," I said, picking up his glass and bringing it up to my mouth.

"Don't!" Dean used whatever energy he had left to knock the glass out of my hand and onto the floor. "This is my freedom *and* my punishment, my life." White foam started to leak out of his mouth between his words. "I love you!"

"I love you too." I kissed his forehead, and before I looked into his face again his eyes were shut. "I can't tell them that you hurt me, baby." I felt his hand tighten around my wrist, asking me to stop being stubborn.

"Dean Tyson, come out with your hands up!" the Coast Guard said again. "Everyone aboard, please come out with your hands in the air."

"I can't do this without you," I said, putting my head on his chest. He tightened his hold on me. "I can't. Don't make me do this alone." This time his grasp tightened but slowly faded and his hand fell from my body. I was on my own.

I looked at the bottle on the bar and listened to the Coast Guard ship calling his name over and over for what seemed like hours, but it was really only a minute or two. I could drink whatever was in the bottle and have instant freedom by death, or I could walk out with my hands up and pretend to be the victim and risk going to prison when my story was torn apart by a few wise detectives.

I kissed Dean good-bye. I walked over to the bar, grabbed the bottle of lethal liquid, and cried as I poured it into a glass. As I brought the glass to my mouth, I looked over at Dean's body and imagined the things people would say about us since we wouldn't have tongues to speak for ourselves. I thought about the madman they would make him out to be, the animal they would call him, the maniac they would introduce him as to the entire world. I couldn't let that happen to him; I needed to tell his story. Destiny deserved to know what kind of man her father really was.

In the midst of my tears I took a deep breath, put down my fatal cocktail, and slowly walked onto the stern of the boat with my hands in the air.